To JoAnn Currie —
A great horsewoman and a
dedicated, caring physical therapist!

Bless Me, Father

Best!

Pennifer

R A

Bless Me, Father

R.J. Peinkofer

Copyright © 2005 by R.J. Peinkofer.

ISBN: Softcover   1-4134-7886-7

All rights reserved. No part of this book may be reproduced or transmitted in any form or by any means, electronic or mechanical, including photocopying, recording, or by any information storage and retrieval system, without permission in writing from the copyright owner.

This is a work of fiction. Names, characters, places and incidents either are the product of the author's imagination or are used fictitiously, and any resemblance to any actual persons, living or dead, events, or locales is entirely coincidental.

This book was printed in the United States of America.

To order additional copies of this book, contact:
Xlibris Corporation
1-888-795-4274
www.Xlibris.com
Orders@Xlibris.com

27359

To my loving wife, Alda, for her vision and care. Special thanks to good friends, Pat Nunn and Virginia Pence for their careful reading of the manuscript, to Alberta Hutchinson for her inspirational art work, and to Bob and Jim Peinkofer for their never-ending support.

Prologue

In the early 1500's when Martin Luther tacked his 95 Theses to the door of his church, he caused a whirlwind. It spread through Germany, Switzerland, France and all the way to England. He challenged all the rules and regulations of the church in Rome. Drastic changes started to occur; new churches arose; attendance at Luther's mass was not compulsory as it was in the Roman Church. With this newfound freedom the peasants followed the example and started to revolt against the principles and all authority. It was a bloody revolt. In many instances, anarchy prevailed.

St. Francis Ignatius started as a page in the court of Ferdinand and Isabella. He was educated and taught the finer points of handling all arms of war. He became a soldier. He was injured during one battle and decided that he would give his life to the church. In 1543 with seven men, he started the Society of Jesus, known as the Jesuits. They took vows of poverty, chastity and obedience. They were to be the defenders of the Roman Catholic Church against all heresy. They were to be the soldiers of Jesus.

At the beginning, the Jesuits were not accepted. It was not until seven years later when they were approved by the Pope that their numbers started to flourish. Not only did they have priests, but brothers who acted as helpers. The princes and leaders of countries put pressure on the Pope not to allow them to expand too far. The Pope issued an edict that the Jesuits were to be active in Russia and Prussia. This curtailed their activity greatly but still they were able to recruit. Cells of the Jesuits formed in various places.

Father Roman led one such cell. He had four priests and 20 helpers or brothers. They found much resistance and living was difficult. Father Roman asked one of his priests, Father Jerome, to meet with him. Father Roman looked at Father Jerome and said, "We must do something to protect our group and our movement. What would you suggest?"

Father Jerome, like St. Ignatius, had been a soldier. He said, "Why not find out who in our band has experience with arms. We could form a small band that would offer protection to us and to others who are faithful to the church."

Father Roman said, "So be it. Why not poll our brothers and see which ones are skilled in the use of arms."

Father Jerome met individually with each member of the group. He found out their skills and their complete backgrounds, noting those strengths that might be useful to the group as a whole. After a number of days he developed a list of seven of the men who had been skilled in the use of arms. With the blessing of Father Roman he took this group off to a wooded area away from the others. Father Jerome stood in front of them and he said, "Who, here, are willing to die for the faith?"

All answered in the affirmative. He asked, "Who here would be able to meet violence with violence?"

All affirmed. "From now on, at any time or any place we as a group are met with violence, we will retaliate. When one of the faithful is being threatened, we will come to that person's aid with the same enthusiasm that the enemy showed to our friend." He continued, "Henceforth, on the inside of your right sleeve will be stitched a red shield, which will identify us to each other."

When they got back to the group, Father Jerome reported what had happened to Father Roman. Father Roman said, "Maybe we can make our journey safer and help those who are faithful to the church."

Father Jerome sought out one in the group who had been a blacksmith. He told him what he wanted and asked if he would be able to achieve the same. The brother said he thought it was possible but he would have to go throughout the countryside to find the materials necessary. Father Jerome said, "Take several other brothers with you so that you are not harmed," and he did.

Chapter 1

When St. Anthony's Church, located outside of Albany, New York, was formed in the early 1900's, the surrounding area was essentially rural. It was in the center of a very small community with homes and stores. The church had been constructed of rough, volcanic-like rock, and was a beautiful building. A two-story yellow brick school building faced the church. Some distance behind the school building there was a red brick convent. To the left of the church was a Victorian-style rectory. St. Anthony's was considered fortunate to have sixteen nuns living in the convent, several of whom still taught at the school. The rest worked throughout the community. Over the years, the city stretched beyond its boundaries and encircled St. Anthony's parish so that now it was considered an inner city church.

Sister Ann Marie rose early, showered, dressed, had a cup of coffee and was about to leave the convent to walk over to the church to prepare for the 6:00 a.m. Mass. Behind the church, at the doorway leading to the sacristy, a large figure loomed. He moved stealthily for a man of his size. He reached up and unscrewed the light over the doorway entrance and stood quietly in the dark. He tore off a 6-inch piece of duct tape from a small roll, which he had in his pocket. He fixed it to the inside of his left hand with the sticky portion outward. He watched Sister Ann Marie leave the convent and walk along the sidewalk toward him. As she neared the doorway, he stepped out, clapped his left hand over her mouth, and pressed the tape firmly in place so that she could not make a sound. With his right hand he held a knife up against her throat and said, "Sister, don't move or you'll die."

He told her to put her arms behind her and when she did he put a loop of rope around her wrists, pulled it tightly, wound the rope and secured it so that she could not use her hands. Over her eyes, he tied what appeared to be a large handkerchief. He put his powerful left arm around her waist and picked her up. Still holding the knife in his right hand, he took her over to a bench and placed her on it. He pushed her back into a reclining position and then with an upward swing of his right arm shoved the knife into her just below her rib cage. He withdrew the knife and wiped it clean on the nun's habit. She was dead within seconds. The attacker then turned and walked toward the cemetery behind the gardens of the church. Soon he was lost in the darkness.

Father Michael O'Malley and his widowed sister, who was his housekeeper, were walking from the rectory to the back of St. Anthony's Church for 6:00 a.m. Mass. Father O'Malley's rotund appearance set off his gentle face. His blue eyes sparkled and he was quick to smile. He was from the old school, so he still wore a cassock. His sister, Martha, was tall and thin. She wore a flowered print dress and, as always for Mass, a dark blue hat.

As the two approached a circular grotto dedicated to the Blessed Virgin, they were astounded to see the figure of a nun in front of one of the benches. She appeared to have fallen asleep on the bench and had rolled off. On closer inspection, they saw that the white collar of her habit was stained bright red.

Father O'Malley knelt down and felt her neck for a pulse. There was none. He uttered, "God have mercy," and turned to Martha. "Call 911 and then tell Father Tom to come quickly!"

While Martha ran back to the Rectory, Father O'Malley reached into his pants pocket, pulled out a stole, put it around his neck and started to say the prayers for the dead: "Eternal rest grant unto her, O Lord, and let perpetual light shine upon her. May she rest in peace. May her soul and the souls of all the faithful departed, through the mercy of God, rest in peace. Amen."

The scene was a paradox: the circular flagstone walkway with a statue of Mary in the center was surrounded by beds of flowers and close-cut grass, now marred by blood and death. Father O'Malley wondered what evil had taken the life of Sister Ann Marie. How long had he known her? For some reason he could not remember. She had come to the convent as a young woman. She studied, became a novice and then took her final vows at St. Anthony's. She had been family. Why, oh why? He continued to pray with the tears rolling down his round cheeks. The usual smile was gone; the sparkle in his eyes was now replaced by a dead-like stare as he gazed at the statue of Mary.

Father Tom Johnson came running down the walk from the rectory. He was wearing jeans and a T-shirt. On his feet were sneakers. He had an athletic look and was very popular with the young people of the church. Due to his efforts participation had increased dramatically in the youth groups. He was thirty-five but looked much younger.

He ran up to Father O'Malley. Seeing the body, he said, "Dear Lord, what happened?"

O'Malley responded that Sister Ann Marie had been killed. Father Tom asked if O'Malley had seen anyone. Father O'Malley explained that he and Martha had found her like this. O'Malley asked his assistant to say the Mass as he just could not do so. Father Tom asked if he would be all right out here. O'Malley said, "Don't worry about me. I'll wait until the police arrive and then meet you inside."

Father Tom put his hand on the older man's shoulder and said, "Okay." He then headed for the sacristy, as it was almost time for Mass to begin.

Soon after, Martha returned and said to her brother, "Come over here and sit on one of the benches." At first he resisted but finally gave in. She said, "Here, drink this coffee. It will help you."

He took the coffee and drank from the cup. Martha sat next to him in the quiet of the grotto. Not only was Martha his sister, but probably his best friend. After her husband died two years ago, Father Mike insisted that Martha come and live with him.

She retired as a skilled office manager eight months ago. At first, not having much to do, she started to tidy up the parish records since she had brought her computer with her. She also kept the financial records and made all the reports to the Diocese. In addition, with the aid of a cleaning person, she took care of the house and cooked the evening meal for the two priests.

After what seemed like an eternity, a strange man, hat in hand, walked toward Martha & Father O'Malley. He was a big man. His hair was rumpled and his suit looked as if he had been sleeping in it. In a quiet tone he said, "Father, may we talk? I am Detective James, Bob James that is."

Father O'Malley responded, "My name is O'Malley and this is my sister, Martha."

Looking over at the body, Detective James asked, "Did you find her?"

O'Malley nodded his head and said, "Yes, we both did."

"Did you touch anything?"

"Only to feel for a pulse in her neck."

Detective James said, "We will have a team here shortly to see what we can find. Is there some place you can go and we will talk later?"

Martha said, "Let's go back to the rectory. I'll fix you something to eat."

Turning to the detective she asked, "Would you like something?"

James said, "Maybe later."

Taking Father O'Malley by the arm, Martha started to lead him off. The priest turned toward James and said, "Call me Father Mike. Everyone else does."

Just after noon, Father Mike was in his study, seated in his favorite recliner. The room had dark paneling with bookshelves covering one wall. The books included everything from novels to religious texts. Father Mike was an avid reader. Near the bay window, which looked out onto the lawn and flowerbeds, was his old mahogany desk. On the desk were several piles of neatly stacked papers.

Across from the desk was a leather couch with a small table in front of it. On each side of the couch were end tables with lamps on them.

There was a knock on the door. Father Mike said, "Come in."

Martha appeared through the door opening and said, "The detectives are here."

He said, "Show them in."

Detective Bob was followed by a very large, handsome, neatly dressed African-American man. Detective Bob said, "Father, this is my partner, Beauregard Washington, but everybody calls him 'Beau'."

Father Mike said, "Glad to meet you, Beau."

He invited them in and they were seated on the couch. Bob, looking at Father Mike, said, "Father, we just want to tell you what we have found. We're afraid it isn't very much."

Presently, Martha came in with a tray of ham and cheese sandwiches, a pot of coffee, cups, napkins, pickles and three slices of apple pie. She put it down on the coffee table in front of the couch and said; "Now gentlemen, enjoy your lunch. Would you care for anything other than coffee to drink?"

Beau said, "I'm kind of coffeed-out. May I have a glass of milk, please?"

Martha replied, "Of course," and left the room.

As he munched on his sandwich, Detective Bob turned his face toward Father Mike and said, "We don't have much evidence. We did find a heel mark and we do have the tape that was over the nun's mouth and the bandanna that was over her eyes. They've all been sent to the lab for testing. The coroner has picked up Sister Ann Marie's body and taken it to the hospital for an autopsy. If you would call the morgue, you could tell them which funeral parlor you wish to have pick her up."

Father Mike looked at them both and said, "Is there any real possibility of finding out who did this terrible thing?"

Beau looked at him and said, "Father, we're going to keep trying, but I must tell you the chances are slim. It's one of those cases where there just isn't that much evidence." He continued,

"Father Tom gave all the information that we need about Sister Ann Marie. We understand that she didn't have any family."

Father Mike said, "No, shortly after she came here, her father died leaving her all alone—no brothers or sisters, and I don't believe even any distant relatives. We're her family. We'll bury her here and have a solemn Mass at church."

Detective Bob said, "Father, have any of the other nuns had any trouble?"

Father Mike said, "I really don't know." Then he said, "Wait a minute." He picked up the telephone and pressed the intercom to the convent. The Sister Superior answered. Father Mike said, "Sister, would it be convenient for all the nuns to gather in the meeting room of the convent?"

Sister Superior said, "Father, as soon as they are finished with their lunch—in about 15 minutes, we'll all get together in the meeting room if you would like to come over."

Father Mike said, "Thank you very much, Sister."

The detectives finished eating the sandwiches. Father Mike said he didn't feel much like eating any food. When they were finished, they walked over to the convent. On the way, Beau said, "This is a very beautiful place."

Father Mike said, "Yes, it is. We've worked hard at making it so. The parishioners, the nuns, our altar boys and all of us have tried to make this a place of beauty and serenity in the heart of the city."

Detective Bob said, "How long has the convent with the nuns been here?"

Father Mike said, "They were here long before I arrived. They teach in our school and a number of them have special projects with the poor throughout the city. They really do good work."

When the three of them entered the front door of the convent, they were met by the Sister Superior. She said, "Gentlemen, welcome, under these very trying circumstances." She led them into a large meeting room. All the nuns were seated around tables. Father Mike sat down. Beau and Bob stood up in front.

Bob asked, "Have any of you had any problems with any person harassing you?"

Sister Felicia raised her hand and said, "We've been talking about that and three of us (motioning to the nuns on either side of her) had a man give us a hard time when we were out on the street the other day."

Bob asked, "What kind of a hard time?"

Sister Felicia responded, "Oh, negative comments like 'Here come the penguins', and 'Have you said your rosary today', things of that nature."

Beau asked, "Were there any sexual connotations to the person's remarks?"

Felicia said, "Not really."

He asked, "Can you describe him?"

She said, "We've talked about that also. Sister Melanie described him as wearing jeans, a white T-shirt, heavy shoes, a blue jacket, and a baseball cap."

Beau asked, "What about height and weight?"

Sister Felicia started to reply but Sister Angelica interrupted with a motion of her hand and Beau asked, "Yes, Sister?"

"Another thing, he had rumpled, dirty-looking black hair that came down over his ears," and she gestured as to the length of the hair.

Sister Felicia interjected, "In answer to your question, Beau, he was a big man, maybe six feet tall and about 180 pounds."

Beau said, "Thank you very much, Sister."

Detective Bob said, "Well, if there's nothing else I think we'll be leaving."

Beau, Father Mike, and he all thanked Sister Superior and the nuns and walked out of the convent.

Father Mike said goodbye to the two detectives and walked back to the rectory. In the kitchen he stopped and had a cup of coffee. When Martha came in, he said, "I'll be going now. I have an appointment with the Bishop to keep him informed on what has happened."

She asked him what time he'd be back, and he said he wouldn't be too long so they could have their dinner at the usual time.

Father Mike drove the parish car to the Diocesan office, walked into the Bishop's secretary's office and announced himself. The secretary picked up the phone and said,

"Father O'Malley is here. Certainly, thank you."

She looked up at O'Malley and said, "You may go right in."

The office was big, beautiful and well appointed. Much of the furniture was leather, and there were rows of books lining the walls. Bishop Owen, a short, balding man, came out from behind his massive desk, with its piles of neatly arranged papers. He stretched out his hand, saying, "Hello, Mike. Sorry to hear the bad news."

Father Mike answered, "Yes, isn't it terrible?"

The Bishop said, "Come, sit down. You know my secretary, Father Ronald, don't you?"

Mike said, "Yes."

Father Ronald was a tall, well built young man who wore dark-framed glasses. He had been standing in a corner, going through a book from one of the shelves. He came forward and shook Father O'Malley's hand. Father Ronald was a Jesuit. The Bishop said, "Tell us about it, Mike."

Father Mike related all that had happened that day and told them that the police had not found much evidence. He expressed his concern for the rest of the nuns and reported that they would try to take precautions, making sure all the lights were lit and that nobody was on the premises who shouldn't be. After a few minutes, he excused himself and left the Bishop's office. The Bishop had offered any help that he could give and Father Mike felt a little better at having talked the whole thing out.

Shortly after Father Mike's departure, the young secretary, Father Ronald, excused himself, walked down the hall to his own small, private office. He sat at his desk, picked up the telephone and dialed a number. He then explained that one of the nuns had been murdered at St. Anthony's. He also reported that several other nuns had been harassed on the street as they were going about their work with the poor. He said, "Can you be of any help?"

The answer was in the affirmative.

"Thank you," he said, and hung up.

Chapter 2

Several weeks went by, and every once in awhile Father Mike got a telephone call from either Beau or Bob. Their efforts to find the man whom the nuns had described were fruitless. They really had no leads but they were still working on the case and would continue to do so. But it didn't look at all hopeful that they would ever find the murderer.

Several months passed and things at St. Anthony's were back to normal. Every morning, one of the nuns would go over to the church to prepare for the six o'clock mass. One morning in early September, Sister Margaret Mary got up, showered, and was putting on her habit. She thought that putting on the hood, the cap, the big white starched collar was a pain, but then, on second thought, she said, "No, this keeps giving the people a sign of whom I am."

She felt very good as she left the convent and started to walk to the church. The flowers were almost gone and the leaves were turning a brilliant hue—red, yellow, light green, mixed among the dark pine needles. It was a nice day and she felt full of life. As she approached the back door of the sacristy, she really didn't notice that the light was out. As she drew closer, a figure stepped out, put a hand over her mouth and pressed something against her neck. A gruff voice said, "Move and you die."

She did not struggle. She could feel something over her mouth like a piece of tape. A gravelly voice told her to put her hands behind her back, which she did. The assailant slipped a noose around her hands, and wound the rope around and up in between her hands and arms so that she was securely bound. He pulled back the hood of her habit and bound her eyes with a cloth. He released her neck, put his arms around her waist from behind, and half-dragged her to one of the benches. He seated her on the bench and was standing over her when he said; "You'd better make your peace with God."

With that, he raised the knife over his head. Before he could do anything else, a calm, quiet voice came out of the dark. The voice said, "I wouldn't do that if I were you. You could get hurt."

The attacker turned in his crouch, looked up and saw a person dressed in black. He raised the knife even higher and started for that person. Before the attacker had moved inches, there was a very quiet pop. All of a sudden, there appeared on the attacker's forehead, a neat, round hole, but the back of his skull was completely blown out. He stopped in his tracks, fell backwards on his side and crumpled onto the pavement. He uttered not a single word. The figure in black put the gun back in a leather holster attached to his belt. He walked slowly to Sister Margaret Mary and said quietly,

"Sister, it's all right. Do not fear. Your attacker is dead. I'm going to help you sit up. Don't worry; it's all right. I'll untie your hands," which he did. He then said to her, "Try to remove the tape from your mouth. I would do it but I don't wish to hurt you."

She got the tape off her mouth and then said, "Whoever you are, thank you."

He said, "Sister, do me a favor. Please do not take off the blindfold until I am gone. Count to twenty and remove it. Then go to the rectory and have them call 911. Have the assistant pastor come out here and stand guard until the police get here so that no evidence is disrupted. You stay in the rectory until the police arrive and come to question you. Answer them honestly. Goodbye and good luck."

The figure in black walked through the church grounds to a car parked on a side street. He got in, started the motor and began to drive away. As he passed under the street light on the corner, his white collar reflected brightly. When he was driving out of town, he saw blinking lights ahead—red and blue. As he approached, he saw a police car and an ambulance. There had been an accident. He stopped, got out and walked toward the car that apparently had crashed into a pole. The car had been totally demolished. The driver's side door looked as if somebody had opened it with a can opener. He knew they'd have to use the Jaws of Life. One of the paramedics saw him and said, "Father, would you come here, please?"

He walked forward and saw a man on the stretcher. One arm and a leg were bent in a very unnatural fashion. The paramedic said quietly, "I don't think he's going to make it. He's been asking for a priest. It's a miracle that you've come along."

The figure in black knelt down beside the man. The man looked into his eyes. The figure in black took out his stole, put it around his neck and led the man through an act of contrition. The man looked at him and whispered, "I feel better now and I'm not afraid. Thank you, thank you."

He closed his eyes, his head rolled to the side and his breathing stopped. The figure in black felt for a pulse. There was none. The paramedic said, "Well, we can take him in now. We won't have to race. You know, I think it's really fantastic you came along. You probably helped him into heaven."

The priest got up, walked to his car slowly while thinking about what the paramedic had said. He thought, "Helped one into heaven, the other into hell."

Chapter 3

Thirty miles south of Albany, New York there is an old monastery a quarter of a mile off the main road. On each side were well-kept lawns and behind the lawns were rows of trees. The place was immaculate. The driveway ended in a circle in front of a large building. In the middle of the driveway were beautiful beds of flowers and in the center was a statue of St. Ignatius Loyola. The large building in front housed the staff, students, a dining hall, meeting rooms and the office. To the right was the chapel and to the left, the library. All the buildings had been constructed more than 100 years ago by skilled artisans and were made of stone found on the property. The chapel had a high, vaulted ceiling with exposed dark beams. The sun shone through the multicolored stained glass windows, which depicted prominent people from the Bible. On the left was the beautifully constructed library with shelves containing hundreds and hundreds of books. The basement under the library had been hewn out of solid rock. At the base of the stairs, leading down from the first floor, was a stout, oaken door. When this was open, another large door could be seen. The first door was always closed before the second was opened. This maintained the climate in the basement.

Along the walls there were shelves that contained boxes of documents, which had been shipped from all over the world—from monasteries, churches, convents and libraries no longer in existence. The reason for this storage of old documents was that the temperature in the basement did not vary more than three degrees from summer to winter, remaining around 50 degrees Fahrenheit.

Seated at desks were two men dressed much alike in jeans, plaid shirts and jackets. Each of the men was reading documents. They had been doing so now for a period of weeks. Father Stephan was a professor at a university and at times taught courses at the Monastery. His field of expertise was church history and languages.

The other man was Dick Rogers, whose stance betrayed his military background. He had been a longtime friend of Father Stephan and spent many hours with him helping to research and catalogue the documents at the Monastery.

Father Stephan was a man of medium stature and build, with white hair and a pointed nose. He was a happy man. Dick was tall and thin. He had been a businessman and was now retired. He loved church history as much as Father Stephan. Dick looked over at Father Stephan and said, "Find anything interesting?"

Father Stephan looked back and wearily groaned, "Not really. This is some stuff from the early exploration days of several Jesuits in America. In fact, it's about the Albany area."

Dick said, "Yes, a lot of that stuff is already documented in books. You know, not only did the Jesuits have a firm belief in education, but also in doing missionary work. There were a few martyrs up in this area, too, I believe."

Father Stephan replied, "Yes, if I remember correctly, two in this area."

"Well," Dick said, "back to work, it will be lunch time soon." He was going through memos, journals, letters and various documents from the 1500's. He'd been reading avidly now for a couple of hours, and all of a sudden he came onto a journal that had a small red shield inscribed on the front cover. He opened it and found that the journal had been kept by a Father Jerome. It recounted the trip Father Jerome and five brothers had taken some distance from their home to a small hamlet where many of the peasants remained true to the Catholic Church. They had walked along the dusty path, each carrying a stave about six feet long. At the top of the stave was a bright brass cross. Around the brothers' middles were tied leather pouches in which they carried their food and other essentials for such a journey. As they traveled, they came upon a thickly wooded area, and after some time, they heard a violent scream. They went very cautiously through the woods, using the larger trees as protection to hide from any danger in front of them. Suddenly they came upon a clearing. In the clearing were several men with swords. They were battling with the peasants who were using only clubs. One man lay on the ground, bleeding profusely. With a nod from Father Jerome, he and the rest of the brothers stepped out into the clearing.

Father Jerome said, "What is happening?"

The biggest man with a sword said, "This is none of your business."

Father Jerome said, "Stop in the name of the Lord."

The big man retorted, "The hell with the Lord. We have no need of you or Him. We are going to finish up our business."

Father Jerome and the brothers grasped their staves in their left hands slightly below the brass crosses. With their right hands, they grabbed the tops of the crosses and pulled. Out came long, slim swords, which sparkled in the sunlight. They engaged the ruffians who were killing the townspeople. Brother John suffered a wound on his upper right arm, and one of the other brothers stepped in to protect him. Father Jerome engaged the big man, who was powerful. However, the big man moved with stealth, and used brute-force in the swordplay, not his brain. Every time the man would thrust, Father Jerome would parry his sword off to one side or the other. Finally, after about 10 minutes, the man came at Father Jerome with a slash. Father Jerome parried, slid his sword along the other man's blade and punctured him through the heart. The man dropped without uttering a word. Others of the ruffians were down and dead. The rest fled. The brothers and Father Jerome set about binding the wounds of the villagers using white cloths they took from the pouches hanging from their belts.

When they were finished, Father Jerome asked one of the men who was still standing with a club in his hands, "What was this all about?"

The man answered, "We were attacked by these hooligans because we are faithful to Rome. We came out to the forest to find wood for our fires, but I don't think we truly showed our strength."

He then looked at Father Jerome and asked, "What are you doing in these parts?"

Father Jerome said, "We have come to bring the Mass to those who are still faithful."

The man looked and smiled as he said, "That is good."

Dick continued to read the inch-thick journal. He found accounts of more and more events where the Jesuits had found violence and had overcome it with violence, but in doing so had saved lives and helped others.

As he put down the journal, Father Stephan said, "Come on, Dick. It's lunchtime." Dick looked at Stephan and said, "Father, read this one when we get back. You'll be surprised."

Meals at the monastery were not fancy. They were just good, solid, and very tasty. Dick and Father Stephan didn't eat too much because of their sedentary lifestyle of working in the library with little or no exercise. Once in awhile they'd go into town for a swim at the YMCA or walk around the beautiful grounds. After coffee and a cigar enjoyed by Father Stephan (it was one of the two he had each day after each main meal), the men walked slowly around the buildings, enjoying the fresh air. When Father Stephan's cigar was finished, they headed back to the library. Back at their desks, Father Stephan took up the journal that Dick had just read, and Dick continued through the pile of documents in the box. On the outside of the box it said, "The 1500's." However, Dick was finding other papers, other accounts of the people of the red shield. A great number of these men had given up their lives to protect others. In times of emergency, they moved in, not really taking into consideration the odds against them. The last sheaf of papers was dated 1943, during World War II.

Dick read about a small island off the coast of France that housed a fishing village. The island was occupied by a contingent of German soldiers. The commanding officer, a Colonel, was a dyed-in-the-wool Nazi in the SS. His behavior was erratic and often brutal. On several occasions he shot his own men for no apparent reason. If anything happened on the island that displeased him, he would take prisoners and either brutally beat or kill them. He even belittled his own assistant, a Major, in front of the troops. One time, in private, the Colonel got so angry, he slapped the Major across the face with his glove. The last straw was when he shot two children who were running across the street, playing in front of his staff car.

The Colonel wanted to take an inspection trip around the island to check on the defenses. The Major knew that this was a stupid idea since nobody would ever invade the island. It was probably the last place with which the Allies would bother. However, he got behind the wheel and started to drive. The Colonel found many things with which he was unhappy. He yelled at the Sergeants and the Lieutenants. Finally they came to a stop on a high cliff above the ocean. Not far away was the village church.

Father Nicholas had been the pastor here for more than 20 years, and he knew everyone on the island and counted them as his friends and family. As they were seated in the car, the Major turned to the Colonel and said,

"There's not much chance of anybody coming here. Not only is this cliff unscalable, but the millrace down below keeps running and thrashing over the rocks almost 24 hours a day. No one could land here and escape the rocks."

Quietly, a figure approached. It was Father Nicholas. He went to the side of the command car where the Colonel was seated. He looked at the Colonel, eyes piercing, wind blowing his long gray hair. He was not a big man. In fact, he was a little on the frail side. He said, "Colonel, the killing will stop. By now you should have had your fill."

The Colonel said, "Major, shoot him."

Without a sound, the priest lifted from the folds of his cassock a nine-millimeter pistol, a German gun. He aimed and pulled the trigger and put a hole right through the Colonel's heart. The priest looked at the Major and said,

"Now you can shoot me. I've done my job."

The Major said, "For what? I will say that the Colonel has had an accident. In his hurry, he drove too close to the edge of the cliff. The ground was soft and the command car went over, taking him while I was talking with you at the church."

The Major got out of the car, went around the back, unfastened the gasoline can. He poured gasoline over the Colonel's body after putting him behind the steering wheel. He poured more gas in the back of the command car. He pushed the command car slightly forward, about 18 inches. As the car's front wheels started to drop through the soft earth, he lit a torch that he'd made by rolling up paper, and threw it into the car. There was a whoosh as the gasoline ignited. The car went over the edge of the cliff, bouncing down on the rocks. When it hit the big rocks below, the gasoline tank exploded and burned. The Major looked down and said, "Just like the fires of hell."

He turned to the priest and said, "Come on, Father. I'll walk you back to your church. I am not the one to judge you. That will come when you face your Maker."

He held out his hand. Father Nicholas extended his right hand to shake the hand of the Major and noticed on the inside of the right cuff of the priest's sleeve, a small red shield.

Dick handed Father Stephan the last pages of the report he had read. He said, "I think you'll find these truly interesting."

While Father Stephan read, Dick busied himself sorting some papers still on the desk. When Father Stephan finished, he turned to Dick and said, "Quite fascinating, isn't it? Who would ever have thought?"

Dick said, "Yes, it is, isn't it? Do you suppose that particular group could be still active today?"

Father Stephan said, "I wonder what would need to be protected today or what violence would need counter-violence to protect the church?"

Dick said, softly and thoughtfully, "You know, during lunch, I was really scanning everybody's sleeve. Maybe my imagination was running away with me, but I thought I saw something on

Father Skinner's sleeve. I don't really know if it was something that was put there or a spot from the spaghetti we had for lunch." He continued, "I think when the time is ripe and we're at the right place, I might approach him on the subject."

Father Stephan said, "Good luck," with a little chuckle. "I don't think Father Skinner is anyone to fool with."

Chapter 4

Empire Realty Company was on the tenth floor of a high-rise office building in the center of the city. In reality, Empire was a holding company for many lucrative enterprises throughout the city, all of them legitimate. It was also the center of operations for almost every illegal enterprise found in the city.

The office was a place to behold. No expense had been spared. It had the latest equipment: a phone system with half a dozen lines, lights perfectly set, a wet bar along one wall that could be concealed by a sliding wall, and overstuffed furniture with magnificent upholstery. To a person walking in it had the appearance of a successful business.

The head of this operation, Angelo Salvador, had died several months before. His eldest son, Manny, took over the business. His second son, Tony, was Manny's first assistant. Manny was short in stature, had a short fuse and a violent temper. Many people suffered as a result of crossing him for the slightest reason. Tony was tall, coolheaded, suave-looking and had black hair that was combed straight back. He really should have been the boss. Manny was yelling at the top of his voice at one of the men who had just brought him a message. He said, "What the hell do you mean that our shipment has been lost?"

The younger man said, "Not lost, boss—destroyed!"

Manny said, "Destroyed? How the hell can it be destroyed? We've got two factories operating down in that banana republic. How the hell can something be destroyed out in the middle of the jungle?"

The younger man, Wally, replied, "Well, the story I hear is that the church has issued bulletins to all its people to help curtail the spread of narcotics. It seems a couple of priests got together and trained some of the Indians in the jungle how to use firearms and explosives. They took them in and knocked out both of our labs. I don't know. We must have lost about two or three tons of cocaine."

On hearing this, Manny became enraged. His face grew red. His hands gestured violently, cutting through the air. Then he screamed, "There it is again—that goddamn church—they ought to be hung. I'm gonna find out who did it and put out a contract."

Wally said, "Boss, we'll never find the Indians—and we're not too sure who the priests were. Besides, we can't put out a contract on a priest."

Manny yelled, "You stupid son of a bitch; if we have to, we'll put out a contract on the Pope! Find out and let me know."

Tony had been sitting quietly at the desk, listening to the tirade. He said gently, "Manny, simmer down. You're not doing yourself any good by screaming and yelling. We'll have to figure out a plan."

Manny said, "Plan, my ass. There's only one way to take care of these things: nip them in the bud." Then, turning to Tony, he continued, "Look, Tony, I've been having enough trouble with the church, much less this sort of thing with them sticking their nose into our business."

Tony thought to himself, "Yep, you've always had problems because you make them yourself."

It seems that Manny had been married for 15 years and had four children. The family didn't much care if Manny took on a mistress or two, but wives and children were sacred. They were never brought into business affairs. They were never used to get back at an individual. Anyone who put his family in jeopardy or abandoned them was not looked upon kindly. There could be some retaliation from the family.

Manny had met a young dancer in one of his nightclubs and had been dating her for quite some time. He wanted to marry her and the only way he could figure out to do so and save his own skin was to get an annulment of his marriage to his first wife. He had applied to the Diocese to obtain an annulment and that was still pending because the application had to go through a marriage tribunal on the Diocesan level. Tony believed, but kept it to himself, that Manny didn't stand much of a chance of obtaining that annulment and trouble was surely brewing in the future, especially with this latest news about the loss of the cocaine. This meant millions on the street.

Chapter 5

In the very private offices on the third floor of the Vatican Office Building, the Secretary of State, Cardinal Joseph Vellini, had gathered two of his advisors and good friends, Frank Salvemini and John Burns. All three were Cardinals. Cardinal Vellini was tall, had thinning gray hair and walked with a stoop. His half-glasses, over which he peered constantly, were perched on the very end of his long nose.

By contrast, Cardinal Burns, an American, was nearly a foot shorter than Vellini and was quite rotund. The third Cardinal, Frank Salvemini, was of moderate height with black, piercing eyes and a hawkish nose. The three were engrossed in a deep conversation about the Pope.

Cardinal Vellini said, "His doctor tells me he is very ill and that he should be moved out of the Vatican and put into intensive care where his food and diet can be monitored; there would be around-the-clock nursing—the works. Also, he is in desperate need of dialysis. If we can obtain this and possibly find a kidney donor, he can have a relatively active life."

Cardinal Burns looked at the other two and said, "When something like that happens the entire organization of the Vatican comes to a standstill. Each day we are faced with many, many problems that must be solved. A lot of those problems are taken to His Holiness for answers."

Cardinal Salvemini said, "Do you think that's really true?"

The Secretary of State said, "Yes, I agree. I think that many departments would hesitate to make decisions, if they feel that the Pope is no longer at the helm and we could lose ground in many areas."

Cardinal Burns asked, "What should we do?"

Cardinal Vellini replied, "Well, we just can't let the poor man go on as he is because as the doctor tells us, he could go into a coma and the good Lord only knows how long he would last. That would mean going through all the ritual it takes to elect a new Pope. Also, we would be very much amiss if we didn't do everything in our power to try to bring him back to health."

After much deliberation Cardinal Salvemini said, "I have an idea. It's weird and I don't know if we can sell it to the Holy Father." He continued, "Is he rational now?"

Cardinal Vellini said, "Yes, he has all his mental capabilities, although he's very weak."

Salvemini continued, "Let's find someone to stand in for him."

Burns looked at him, surprised, and said, "You mean a look-alike for the Pope?"

Salvemini said, "Yes, in a way. If we could find someone of the same stature who looks much like the Pope and has a lot of his background and education, we might be able to pull it off. Of course, no one but the three of us and the person we're obtaining, would know about it."

The Secretary of State said, "How would we go about finding such a person?"

Salvemini said, "Well, I've been thinking. The greatest broad-based clergy we have are in the United States. Perhaps if we contacted select Bishops to find such a person, we might be able to do it."

Cardinal Burns asked, "But how?"

Salvemini said, "We could send a letter. First we would pick a small group of Bishops in areas where we might find the person we're seeking. We'll state in the letter that we would just like to find someone who looks like the Pope and could stand in for him on public appearances because the Pope needs an operation that's not really serious. He'll need someone while he's recuperating—you know, to stand on the balcony, bless the crowds, and that sort of thing. We don't have to be too explicit."

Cardinal Vellini said, "How would we approach the Holy Father? Would we find such a person first or seek his permission first?"

Cardinal Salvemini said, "Let's find the person first. We'll put out the letter and write to three Bishops. I've already settled in my own mind where we would go. Let's do the east coast of the United States and see where we go from there."

The Secretary of State asked, "What's your opinion?" All agreed that this was the avenue to take. Cardinal Burns said, "You said that he might need a kidney transplant to survive?"

Cardinal Vellini said, "Yes."

Burns continued, "Then we should search among the Vatican clergy, within our own people here, and find at least three who have the same blood type so that the doctor can do the tests necessary to see if they might be possible kidney donors."

The other two agreed.

Cardinal Burns said, "All right, I'll take that on as a project. I will contact the Pope's doctor and we can proceed with this."

Chapter 6

Manny and Tony were together in their office at Empire Realty. They were checking over the day's receipts from their illegitimate operations. The secretary knocked at the door, entered, and handed Manny the morning mail.

Manny threw several of the letters over to Tony, saying, "I think these are yours." Manny noted a letter with a return address from the Vatican. He hurriedly tore open the envelope and started to read, when he yelled out, "That no good son-of-a-bitch!"

The marriage tribunal in Rome had turned down Manny's appeal for an annulment. The reason given was the length of his marriage and the number of children. The Vatican could find nothing amiss with his original marriage contract. Manny's wife had fulfilled her part of the contract and so had he; therefore, an annulment was out of the question. They communication further stated that if he obtained a civil divorce and then remarried he would be excommunicated. Manny jumped up screaming at the top of his voice, swearing at everybody and everything in the Catholic Church.

He said, "Excommunication in the family would be just like shooting my own wife! Hell, I'd put a contract out on her tomorrow if I could, but you know I can't, Tony."

Tony looked at him and said, "Manny, don't talk like that. Remember, this is business and you don't do anything to screw up business."

Manny said, "That goddamn Pope. I'm gonna put a contract out on him if it's the last thing I do." In a loud voice he yelled out, "Wally, get in here!"

Wally obediently entered the room and listened as Manny ranted, "Wally, I want you to find a person to take up a contract." Wally said, "On whom?" Manny answered, "The Pope. Who the hell do you think?"

Wally began to stutter but Manny said, "Do what I tell you to do or somebody will have your head." Wally walked out talking to himself. The next day, Wally reported back. Manny asked, "How did you do?" Wally answered, "Boss, nobody will take the contract."

Manny said, "How much did you offer?" Wally replied, "Two hundred and fifty thousand." Manny said, "Go to half a million."

"Nobody will take it at any price," replied Wally. Manny asked, "Have you contacted any of the boys in Chicago or any other place?"

Wally replied, "Yes, but nobody's talking. No one wants any part of this."

Manny was furious. He said, "Hell, you can't even get anybody eliminated any more." Wally said, "Boss, if you really want this we can see what we can find in Europe."

Manny said, "Do it." As word circulated, none of Manny's underlings approved of the proposed contract to put a hit out on the Pope.

Several days later three men appeared at Wally's office, wanting to see him. The three were extremely well dressed in expensive, dark suits. They introduced themselves to Manny's secretary, Carol. She, in turn, picked up the intercom and said,

"Boss. There are three gentlemen here to see you."

Manny responded, "Who are they?"

Carol replied, "Mr. Ronzoni, Mr. Bertuzzi, and Mr. Salvador."

A scowl came over Manny's face as he wondered, "What the hell do they want?" Each of these men enjoyed the same position as Manny in their own organizations. Manny rose from his desk, opened the door to his office and invited the three visitors in. After they were seated, Manny said, "Gentlemen, what may I do for you?"

After exchanging pleasantries, Salvador, with a very stern face, looked Manny directly in the eyes and said, "Manny, we believe that you are skating on very thin ice."

Manny replied, "What do you mean?"

Bertuzzi said, "Manny, we don't take contracts out on the Pope."

Manny's face turned bright red as his anger rose. He said, "You can't tell me what to do. It's none of your damn business!"

Bertuzzi said, "Ah, but you're wrong, Manny. It *is* our business. If you proceed with this, it will pit the whole world against us. We will be guilty by association."

Manny replied, "This is my business. It is personal and I will do as I wish."

Ronzoni stood and the other two followed as he coldly said in a very strong voice, "Manny, do as you will, but you may have to pay the price."

All three then turned and walked out of the office.

Chapter 7

Following their usual habits, Father Stephan and Dick left the monastery on Friday afternoon. If Dick had no business that evening he usually had dinner and spent the night in Father Stephan's home. They were seated in the living room enjoying their coffee with a small glass of brandy. Around the fireplace were five easy chairs facing into a semicircle. Father Stephan was seated to the left of the fireplace and Dick in one of the comfortable chairs facing him. Over the mantle was a large portrait. Dick looked at the picture and then at Father Stephan and he said, "You know, Stephan, if you would cut off that mop of hair you have and lose a couple of pounds, you'd be a dead ringer for the Pope."

Father Stephan chuckled, "I think that not only are your eyes going bad, but also your brain. He's a handsome fellow."

These two men had been friends for many years. They originally met during the Korean War. Father Stephan was a chaplain in the Army, and Dick was attached to Army Intelligence. As a matter of chance, they had shared a tent at Regimental Headquarters Area. There they found that they shared many of the same ideas about life and soon they were fast friends. They were returning to their tent after being up almost all night. Father Stephan was out ministering to a group of wounded soldiers who had been brought into the hospital. Dick had been out gathering information on the battle that had transpired, to find out about all the details so he could make a report to the Regimental Commander. Dick was exhausted and he looked at Father Stephan and said, "I'm not even going to take off my clothes."

Father Stephan said, "Neither am I. I'll get some sleep, then shower and change later in the morning."

They both flopped down on their beds. Not three minutes later there was an explosion that caused a ringing in their ears. Their tent was next to a small hill. The grenade had been tossed into a rather deep depression on the side of a hill. When the grenade went off, most of the shrapnel went upward, tearing holes and ripping the top of their tent to shreds. One fragment of the grenade found its way into the fleshy part of Father Stephan's leg. Another hit Dick in the upper arm. The men were stunned. Father Stephan looked at the top of the tent and said, "Good Lord, if we'd been standing, we now would be dead."

Dick said, "Come on Father, my jeep's right out here. Let's take a drive over to the hospital."

As Dick pulled up to the entrance of the large hospital tent, both he and Father Stephan looked as though they had been through a meat grinder. Dick's pant leg and sleeve, where he had rested his arm while driving one-handed, were covered with blood. Father Stephan's pant leg was completely soaked in blood. A young soldier was standing at the entrance. As they drove up, he didn't know what to do—salute, or run for help.

Dick said to him, "Come on, and give me a hand with my friend." With Dick on one side of Father Stephan and the soldier on the other, they helped him into the entrance. The nurse at the desk yelled for an orderly. She said, "Get help and two gurneys here immediately!"

Both men were placed on the gurneys and wheeled to the treatment area. There were several doctors in attendance. Although their wounds were not life threatening, they were bleeding profusely. The nurses cut away Dick's shirt and Father Stephan's pant leg to expose the wounds. They were each given injections of morphine and a tetanus shot. The doctors removed the fragments that were not too deep and stitched up the wounds. One doctor looked at Father Stephan's collar and saw the cross. He said,

"You know, clergymen are not supposed to get shot or injured." Father Stephan chuckled and said, "I know that, but sometimes we don't know who our enemies are over here. Maybe I'd better cut back on my sermon length at Mass."

They were told that they would have to remain in the hospital for several days because of their blood loss. The doctor said, "Besides, you two look as if you could use some rest."

After three days, they returned to their newly replaced tent and their duties. Father Stephan took his responsibilities very seriously and many times could be found up near the front lines, in battalion aid stations or in company headquarters. He became very popular with the average soldier.

Dick built a good reputation on obtaining and analyzing data about the enemy. Both were promoted from First Lieutenant to Captain. When their tour was completed, Dick returned to the States and then was assigned to Europe. He spent much time in Paris, London and Berlin. While he was still in the Army, he spent most of his time in civilian clothes. The range of his inquiries spanned not only the KGB but various other groups throughout his working area.

Father Stephan returned to his home parish but then was assigned to Catholic University in Washington, D.C., where he worked on his Ph.D. in languages and church history.

* * *

Their coffee and brandy finished, both were content after having Mrs. Jameson's wonderful meal. Father Stephan was reading his breviary; Dick was reading a mystery novel. Once in awhile, Dick would look at Stephan and then at the picture of the Pope. He said to himself, "I'm right. He could be a dead ringer."

After awhile, Father Stephan closed his book, looked over at Dick and said, "What are you reading?" Dick replied, "A very good murder mystery. It seems somebody is killing off the administrative hierarchy in Detroit. It's very interesting, has quite a bit of church history in it, and right now I'm at a part where two Cardinals are discussing the possibility of the marriage of priests. Do you think it will really ever happen, Stef?"

Father Stephan said, "Well, I understand some clergy who are married and converting to Catholicism may remain married. However, if their spouses die, they cannot remarry." He continued, "I don't think there's a broad enough sample yet to come to any firm conclusions. However, I do think eventually the Catholic Church must recognize the fact that if they don't allow priests to marry, our numbers are going to dwindle."

Dick said, "What about females being ordained?"

Father Stephan said, "Not for a long, long time. Probably, though not in my lifetime, priests will be allowed to marry."

Dick looked at Father Stephan and said, "What do you think about the material we found at the monastery?"

Stephan answered, "You mean the stuff with the red shield?"

Dick replied, "Exactly. Do you really believe they existed?"

Father Stephan looked very serious as he said, "You know the Catholic Church went through very trying times all through its history: early persecutions, killings, burning of churches. I can see where it might have been true, especially in the counter-reformation. The general population ran rampant. There was a lot of blood letting. There were martyrs."

He continued, "You know, the early Popes used to take their army out and fight for their lands. They would actually be in battle. So I can understand their attempts to protect the church."

"But do you really think it exists today?" asked Dick.

Stephan said, "I really don't know, but maybe we can find out. I don't think, though, that information would be for publication."

At last, Dick said, "Well, everything in its time. What are you going to do tomorrow?"

Father Stephan said, "I have some papers to go over, I want to check out a few things in my textbooks and pretty much spend tomorrow afternoon in a leisurely fashion."

Dick said, "I'll tell you what I'm going to do. How would you like to have Chinese food tomorrow night for dinner? Your housekeeper usually goes at noon, doesn't she?"

Father Stephan said, "Yes, she does."

"Well," said Dick, "let's go out for dinner tomorrow night."

Stephan said, "All right." He looked at Dick and said, "What are you going to do?"

Dick said, "Well, I think I'll stop in at the Youth Center and maybe check in with one or two buddies of mine. Then I'll go back to the apartment tomorrow afternoon, collect my mail and see what's on the answering machine. Later I'll take a shower, change into some casual clothes and return and pick you up for dinner. Is six okay?"

Father Stephan said, "Good enough."

Just then the grandfather clock in the corner of the room struck a quarter of eleven. Dick said, "Well, shall we?"

Father Stephan said, "Why not?"

Both went off to bed.

Father Stephan was the first one down in the morning. His housekeeper already had the pancakes, bacon and orange juice on the kitchen table with fresh coffee. The aroma of the coffee filled the kitchen. A few minutes later Dick walked in and said, "Good morning."

Father Stephan said, "I thought we were going to have to wake you up today."

"No, no."

They enjoyed their breakfast, making small talk about various things in the news. When they were finished Dick said, "I'll see you about 5:30," and went out, got in his car and drove to the center city.

Chapter 8

Dick had stayed with Army Intelligence for a number of years after Korea and even after he resigned his commission, he was hired from time to time as a consultant on special intelligence affairs. He had the kind of mind that could pick out the relevant details of a problem and a unique ability with mathematics. He became very interested in the early computers as they broke in the so-called modern generation. Over a period of time, he developed and sold several programs that were useful to the various intelligence agencies to which he was connected. When he retired by virtue of wise investments, royalties, pensions and so forth, he was quite well-to-do. He remembered his early, very poor beginnings and as a result started some programs in the inner city. One was the youth center. Dick was well known on the street and liked by almost all the people in the area. Not only did the youth center have as a part of their program such things as basketball, crafts, and the usual sports, but also present were several counselors and tutors to help kids advance in school. Many youngsters took great pride at working on computers in the special room where they received help in languages, math, social studies and history. If it had not been for the center, many of these kids would have dropped out of school.

As he walked through the halls of the center, many kids passing by cheerfully said, "Hello, Mr. Dick!"

That is what they called him. Everybody did.

He knocked on Steve Jones' door. Steve was the director of

the center and was totally responsible to Dick and the Board of Directors. Steve said, "Come on in," and Dick did so.

Dick looked at Steve and said, "I just stopped in for a minute. How are things going?"

Steve replied, "Very well. We just got another grant, a new one, from the federal government. I think our finances are taken care of for the rest of the year."

Dick looked at him and said, "Good work. I appreciate knowing we are sound for a while at least," with a chuckle in his voice.

"Yes, it is always a fight, isn't it?" answered Steve.

Dick asked, "Is there anything I can do for you?"

Steve said, "No, I do not think so."

Dick said, "Well, I'll be off. I want to see some people out on the street."

He walked down several blocks and stopped in front of a storefront restaurant. Above it was a sign, "The Blue Butterfly." He chuckled to himself and went in.

He picked a table not too far from the counter and sat. Almost immediately an elderly gentleman was at his elbow. He said, "How are you doing, Mr. Dick?"

Dick looked at him and said, "Hi, Sam, how are you?"

Sam asked, "What can I do for you today?"

"Sam, the usual."

"Yessir, it will be right up!"

Dick thought to himself that this place truly had the best roast beef sandwich on a hard roll that he had ever tasted. On the roast beef was spread a little horseradish (hot, was that horseradish hot!) Along with that came a nice bottle of non-alcoholic beer. Sam brought two roast beef sandwiches and two bottles of non-alcoholic beer and sat across from Dick. Sam knew that Dick was a diabetic and could not drink regular beer. However, he also knew that Dick liked the taste of beer with his roast beef sandwich. Dick bit into his sandwich, chewed for a few seconds and then said, "This is great!"

Sam looked around the room to make sure nobody had come

in, leaned toward Dick and said, "I have a message for you. You know Manny Salvador, don't you?"

Dick answered, "Yes."

Sam continued, "Well, you also probably know he doesn't have his head screwed on too tight. It seems he's been having (in his mind) some troubles with the Catholic Church. Two priests and a bunch of Indians from Central America knocked off two of his cocaine factories and that ticked him off. He also has been trying to get an annulment from his wife so he can get together with a dancer he picked up. You know the family would not stand for a divorce, so he's really been pressuring the Church. He tried for an annulment with the Diocese and they turned him down. Then he tried again with Rome—he appealed—and they turned him down. This made him livid. All of his life when anything went wrong, he solved it by getting rid of people or beating them up. Now he thinks the Pope is at fault. I don't have to tell you but recently the Church has really come out strongly against drugs, putting as much pressure as is humanly possible on law enforcement and anybody else to control the situation. The other day I had a visit from one of his boys who's quite high up in the Mafia, and he was not too happy with what Manny proposes: putting out a contract on the Pope. The guy who came in knows you and I are friends and that you usually visit here on Saturdays. So he told me that I should tell you what Manny has in mind and maybe through your contacts with the Church you can stop him from doing such a horrible thing."

Dick looked at Sam in disbelief and said, "You mean this is for real?"

Sam said, "Yes."

Dick asked, "How can he get away with such a thing? The family should be on his back!"

Sam looked at him and said, "You know how it works. He's number one and as long as nobody can tie him to anything, he's home free."

Dick said, "Surely a lot of people will know about this?"

Sam said, "I doubt it. The guy who told me is taking his life in his hands. If Manny ever found out, he'd bury him somewhere. That's the way it works. The guy who came in is a good Catholic, even though he's in a dirty business. He figured if he got the word to you, you could do something about it, and maybe that would make up for some of the evil he's done."

Dick said, "Well, I'll have to think about it and pass the word along to the best person or people." He ate in silence for a while and when they finished, Dick stood up, paid his bill and said, "Thank you, Sam. Take care of yourself and don't get in the middle."

Sam said, "Don't worry, I won't."

Dick walked up the street, stopping at several places to renew acquaintances with old friends. He got in his car, went home, checked his mail, showered, changed, and was on his way to Father Stephan's home.

Stephan was seated on his porch waiting for him. When Dick pulled into the drive, Stephan came to the car and got in. He said, "Boy, I'm ready for that Chinese food!"

Dick agreed.

Chapter 9

Sister Margaret Mary was out of breath when she reached the door of the rectory. She knocked and burst through, startling Martha. Sister Margaret Mary said, "Martha, hurry up. Call 911 and get the police here. A man attacked me and now he is dead just outside the sacristy door. I don't know who killed him!"

Martha went immediately to the phone and dialed. When Martha was finished with the phone call, she took Sister in and sat her on a comfortable chair. Father Mike, hearing the noise upon her entry, had heard half of what she said. He looked at Martha and said, "Martha, why don't you get her a cup of coffee. I'll get some brandy."

He went over to the cupboard, got out the brandy bottle, poured a small glassful, and handed it to the nun, saying, "Sister, sip this slowly."

Martha soon had a cup of coffee on the table next to the nun. Father Mike said, "Sister, try to relax and then you can tell us about it."

The sister finally got her breath and had several sips of her coffee, which seemed to revive her. She told Father Mike and Martha about how the man had grabbed her from behind, put the tape around her mouth, covered her eyes and tied her up. She said, "When he threw me down on the bench I did not know what was going to happen. Then a kind soft voice said, 'Do not worry, you are all right.'"

She then told how she was untied, took the tape off her mouth, and waited to take off the blindfold. When she had it off, she ran to the rectory.

Sister Margaret Mary continued, "I did not even look at the man who was lying on the ground. I got here so fast, just as I was told!"

"Sister," said Father Mike, "you just try to stay calm. Martha will fix you some breakfast. I am sure the police will want to talk with you."

He walked over through the hallway to the base of the stairs leading to the second floor and yelled in a loud, firm voice, "Jim, can you come down here a minute?"

Father Jim came bounding down the stairs, looking at Father Mike questioningly, and over at Sister Margaret who seemed a bit disheveled. Father Mike nodded toward the door and they left the rectory.

Once outside, Father Mike told the younger priest what had happened. Father Jim said, "Good Lord, Father, when is it going to end?"

Father Mike responded, "It just well may have."

They walked to the area of the back door of the sacristy. There on the ground was the body of an unkempt man. On the bench was a red bandanna and a piece of duct tape. The attacker lay on the ground, on his back, with his knees drawn up almost in a fetal position. In the middle of his forehead was a neat round hole. Sticking out from under one leg was the blade of a knife. Father Mike said, "Let's not get too close so as to interfere with any evidence."

About four minutes later, a car drove up into the yard of the rectory and parked in front of the garage. Beau and Bob got out, walked over, and said good morning to the priests. The priests returned their greeting. Beau looked at Father Jim and said, "This is a heckuva way to renew an acquaintance."

Father Jim responded, "It surely is."

Both the detectives took out their notebooks and started writing a description of the area, the body, and where various pieces of evidence were. Bob said to Father Mike, "How's the nun?"

Father Mike said, "She's quite shaken up. I imagine you'll be wanting to talk with her."

Bob agreed, "Yes, as soon as the forensic boys are done. They'll be here shortly and so will the coroner."

Several nuns were walking along the path from the convent to the church. Father Mike said to Father Jim, "Will you go explain things to them?"

Father Jim said, "Okay," and went to meet the approaching group. He explained to the Sister Superior and asked her if she would tell anyone coming into Mass that there had been a problem and Mass would be a little late. She said she would and they proceeded around the front of the church.

Father Jim walked back to Father Mike. He said, "Father, I think it would be best if you'd stay with Sister Margaret, and I'll get changed, come back and say Mass."

Father Mike said, "Okay, and thank you very much."

Father Jim had just gone in the back door of the rectory when a car drove up with two men inside, followed by a large, black station wagon. Father Mike assumed this was the coroner. They came out and Beau introduced the two detectives as Detectives Smith and Brody. He introduced the coroner as Dr. Jameson. Bob said to Father Mike, "These are two characters—one English, one Irish. You've got to be careful with these guys."

Brody looked at Bob and said, "Father, these are two ethnic guys. They really are minorities."

Bob had been born Roberto Rodriguez. He lived in the barrio with his family. His father at times had worked two or three jobs. Because of his lack of English and education, all he could obtain were entry-level positions. When Roberto was six, his mother and father were killed in an automobile accident. A drunk driver had run a stop sign and demolished their car. His maternal grandmother had married a man who was a farmer in upstate New York. She and her husband took young Roberto in and later adopted him, and changed his last name to James.

Beau was born and raised in the ghetto. He was always an inquisitive boy, wanting to learn things. A man who operated a grocery store in the neighborhood took a liking to Beau and hired him to do chores around the store such as cleaning up and stocking shelves. As he grew older, he was allowed to wait on the customers and make change. He always encouraged Beau to study and to stay in school. Beau could remember him telling him a thousand times, "Without an education you are nothing! Once you get something in your brain, nobody can take it away from you."

About a month before Beau graduated from high school the old man died. Mr. Schwartz, the proprietor of the store, had left a considerable amount of money in his will for Beau with the stipulation that he go to college. Beau did, deciding that he wanted to study criminology with the goal of becoming a policeman. That was 13 years ago and Beau had become quite successful in his job.

Detective Smith took pictures of the area and the body from all angles. When he was finished, he put the camera on the bench. He and Brody started to pick up the evidence: the rope, the tape, the bandanna, and place them each in separate plastic bags. They sealed and tagged them.

The coroner had knelt down to try to feel a pulse. Feeling nothing, he turned to the detectives and said, "He's dead."

At this pronouncement, Smith and Brody straightened the man's leg. Brody very carefully picked up the knife, put it into a plastic bag, sealed and tagged it. The coroner walked over to his car and brought back what looked like a long piece of plastic. With the help of the detectives, he rolled the body on its side and placed the plastic on the ground. They then rolled the body onto the plastic, pulled up the sides and closed the long zipper that ran the full length of the bag. The three of them carried the body to the back of the black station wagon. After putting the body on a stretcher, they closed the door.

The coroner walked back and said to Bob, "I'll have his personal effects in about an hour. We ought to be able to have everything fingerprinted and take all the samples we need for lab tests, so that when you get over there we can turn the evidence over to you."

Bob said, "Okay. See you later."

The coroner went back to his station wagon, the two men to their car, and all three left the area. Beau said, "Can we talk to the nun now, Father?"

Father Mike said, "Yeah, come on."

They walked off to the rectory. When the entered the house where Sister Margaret was seated, she looked calmer than when Father Mike had left her. The three men walked in and Father Mike introduced them to Sister Margaret.

Beau began, "Sister, can you tell us what happened?"

She told her story as best she could.

Bob asked, "Sister, did you see the man?"

"No, I couldn't. My eyes were blindfolded," replied Sister Margaret.

Beau said to her, "Did you see the man who helped you?"

She replied, "No. Again, my eyes were still blindfolded. He asked me to leave it on, and I did. He had such a kind, gentle voice."

Bob asked if she could give any impression of the man—any feelings she had.

She said, "Not really, but for some reason I think he was tall. I've told you he was gentle and had a quiet, calming voice. As he untied my ropes, he told me everything would be all right."

Bob said, "Well, Father, I think that's all for now. We'll go see what we can find out."

They got up, shook hands with the priest, thanked the nun and left for their car.

Father Mike looked at the nun and asked, "Sister, how are you feeling?"

She replied, "Much better."

"Why don't you go over to the convent and rest."

"Father, I would like to go to Mass and thank the Lord that everything turned out all right."

"Fine," said Father Mike, "but after that I want you to take it easy for today. All right?"

"Yes, thank you, Father," and she left.

Chapter 10

Detectives James and Washington got in their car and started to head toward the center of the city where the morgue was located. They had gone about six blocks when Bob said to Beau, "I haven't had any breakfast. There is a donut place up here. Let's stop and get something to eat and a cup of coffee."

Beau said, "Okay."

They pulled into the donut shop and each ordered two donuts and a cup of coffee. They took breakfast over to a table by the window and sat down.

Beau said, "You know, if we can tie this one to the original murder we can close out the case."

Bob said, "Yes, if the wound on the original victim fits the contour of the knife."

They finished their coffee and donuts, paid the cashier, got into their car and again started for the city morgue. The morgue was in the basement to the rear of an old building that housed many city services. They pulled into the parking lot and entered.

As they walked down the hall, Beau said, "My God, this is a dingy hallway. Look at the paint peeling!"

Bob said, "Yeah, the hallway's not too good, but they have refurbished the labs and the morgue itself completely."

They knocked on the office door marked *Coroner*. A voice said, "Come in."

They opened the door and Beau said, "Hi, Doc. Got anything for us?"

The coroner looked at them and said, "Well, I checked the original photograph, my drawing and my notes and yes, you lucked out. The knife conforms to the wound on Sister Anne, so I would say we have a tie-in with this guy on the original murder. Also, Pete has some news for you over at the forensic lab."

Bob said, "Okay, Doc, thanks very much. We'll go over and talk to him."

On their way down the hall, they stopped at the door marked *Forensic Laboratory* and went in. As they entered the brightly lit, immaculate white room, they saw Pete leaning over and looking into a microscope on the counter top.

Beau said, "Hi, Pete!"

At first Pete did not respond. He finished what he was doing, looked up and smiled, "How are you fellows doing?"

Beau said, "We're doing well."

Pete said, "I think you'll even do better. Remember the first murder case when we unfolded the bandanna and found some seeds. Well, in checking out the pockets of this guy, the same seeds were found."

Bob asked, "What kind of seeds are they?"

"Would you believe, bird feed?"

"Where the heck would he get bird feed?"

Pete said, "Well, he either was a bird lover, which I doubt, or worked some place that sold it."

He looked at Bob and said, "The rest of his stuff is over on the counter. Check it out. It's all been dusted. Oh, by the way, we also found his prints on the knife handle and on part of the blade."

Beau and Bob walked over to the counter. Beau picked up the man's wallet, flipped it open and there, as big as life was his driver's license with a picture: John O'Neill, 119 Fairview Avenue. Bob wrote down the name and address in his notebook, looked at Beau and said, "Well, let's go!"

As they were leaving, they thanked Pete for his good work.

Beau said, "You know, Bob, you were right. The offices are fantastic. It's this stupid hallway I don't like."

They got into the car and headed south toward Fairview Avenue. They were driving down Central when Bob said, "I think it's the next street to the left."

He made the left hand turn. This area of the city had seen better days and as they drove down Fairview, they could see that the houses were very shabby. Beau started checking the numbers of the houses and buildings. There would be a house, an empty storefront, a rundown store. As he clicked off the numbers, finally he said, "There, up on the left, that big brownstone."

The brownstone was only four stories high but it occupied more than two lots. It looked incongruous to the buildings beside it—big and squat. They pulled up across the street, got out, looked up at the building. The white paint was peeling off of the windows. Way up on the fourth floor, two windows were boarded up. They walked over to the door and entered. They checked the mailboxes and found that the super lived in 1-C. They walked down the hallway to the door and knocked. Finally a chain jangled and the door was opened. A skinny little guy with rumpled hair and three days growth of beard said, "Yeah?"

Bob showed him his shield and identification and said, "Police. Do you have a John O'Neill living here?"

The guy said, "Yup."

Bob said, "Will you please get his key and come with us and open his door?"

The skinny little man said, "I don't think I can do that. It's not right. Besides, he's not home right now."

Beau said, "We know that. Now if we need to do it we can get a court order, or we can go upstairs and kick the door down. You can be responsible for fixing it."

The man said, "Well, if you guys are cops, I guess it's all right."

He walked across the room to a board nailed onto the wall. On it were little cup hooks and on each hook was a key—one for each room in the apartment complex. He took the key off the board and walked toward the stairs. They all walked up to O'Neill's apartment. The super unlocked the door, and Beau said, "Okay, thank you. You can go now."

They opened the door and walked to the center of the room. It was a fairly large living room. To the left were a small kitchen and a bath. To their right were two bedrooms. In front of them was a large window. They looked around the room. There were a TV, couch, and two comfortable chairs. The upholstery on the furniture was well worn. Bob said to Beau, "Look over in the corner."

In the corner was a table with a blue cloth draping all the way to the floor. About five feet above the table there was a portico made of the same cloth but tied in intervals with a white cloth. In the center of the table was a large statue of the Virgin Mary. In front of her were six vigil lights and on each side was a vase with dried flowers.

Bob said, "Looks like a shrine, doesn't it?"

Beau replied, "It sure does."

Bob said, "You know I think that's carrying it just a little far."

Beau said, "Well, no telling what people will do."

Paradoxically in the other corner, on the wall was a shield. Under the shield were crossed swords and on each side were four knives. The blades of two of the knives curved back and forth like a snake. One of the knives looked to be a scimitar, curved with the cutting edge on the inside of the curve. Bob looked at Beau and said, "Can you figure it out? Over on the one corner are implements of death and in the other corner, peace."

They checked out the bathroom, the kitchen and both bedrooms. After a little while, Beau said, "Hey, Bob, come here. I want to show you something." He was standing in front of the open door of a large closet. In the closet were women's dresses. All the dresses were black. On one end, the neatest thing in the whole apartment was a nun's habit. A clear, plastic bag covered it, as if it had just been returned from the cleaners. They knew this was not true because the plastic all through the top was covered with dust. They walked out of the bedroom and were startled to see an old lady standing inside the doorway. Her snow-white hair needed combing. She wore a full apron stained with many different things.

She looked at them and said, "Who are you?"
Beau replied, "The police."
She said, "So, he finally got into real trouble."
Beau said, "Who do you mean?"
She answered, "The guy that lives here. He's a real pain, always making fun of people, always nasty."
Bob said, "Do you know his name?"
She said, "Sure, O'Neill. John O'Neill. He used to live here with his mother."
Beau said, "Where's his mother?"
She said, "She died a little over a year ago."
Beau said, "How long have you lived here?"
She said, "Twenty-five, twenty-six years."
He continued, "How long did you know the O'Neills?"
She said, "Twenty years."
Beau said, "What kind of family were they? How about the husband?"
The old lady said, "There was no husband. She never married. What kind of family? Not good. His mother used to belt him around all the time. She kept telling him what a no-good he was, that he'd never amount to anything, that he'd ruined her life."
Bob said, "She really beat up the kid?"
The old lady said, "One time, he did something wrong and she made him kneel on a broomstick and say the Rosary out loud. I could hear him right through the wall!"
Beau asked her, "Did she always wear black clothes?"
The old lady said, "Yes . . . yes," as if she were thinking. "She used to tell a story or something about how she was going to be a nun."
Bob asked, "Does he have any relatives?"
The old lady said, "Yes, his grandmother lives two blocks down."
Bob said, "Do you know the address?"
The old lady said, "I think it's 210."
Beau asked, "What's her name?"
The old lady looked at him and said, "O'Neill, Mrs. O'Neill."

Chapter 11

Secretary of State Cardinal Vellini, Cardinal Burns and Cardinal Salvemini met with the Pope's doctor. Cardinal Vellini asked, "How is His Holiness, Doctor?" The doctor said, "Not good. I have him on strong antibiotics and his kidneys are not doing very well. Soon they will put him on dialysis. However, that cannot be done here in his quarters."

Cardinal Vellini asked the other two men in red how the search for a stand-in was progressing. Cardinal Burns said that the letters had gone out to the United States but no word as yet had been received.

"Soon there will be word, I hope," said Vellini.

Doctor Santos said, "I have checked the medical records of the clergy in the Vatican and have found three that are a match for his Holiness. I called them in and took blood samples. All three candidates were good. However, one was a perfect match."

"Who is he?" asked Cardinal Salvemini.

"He is an Irishman named Sean O'Connor."

With a big smile on his face, Cardinal Burns said, "If we use him we might have to create a Basilica in Dublin."

The other three chuckled.

Vellini said, "I will talk to him."

Dr. Santos asked, "When will you talk to His Holiness?"

Cardinal Vellini said, "It is too late this evening. I will see him in the morning before I see the priest."

The doctor said, "I have a good, small hospital in the north. It is fully equipped. I have two surgical teams on standby. They are Americans and can be here on 24 hours notice. They do not know who the patient is, as yet. I told them that he is an important member of the Vatican."

The next morning, Cardinal Vellini knocked on the door to the Pope's quarters. A young priest, who acted as the Pope's attendant, opened the door and said, "Good morning, your Eminence."

Vellini entered and was shown to the Pope's bedroom. The Pope was still in bed having just finished breakfast. Vellini said, "Good morning, your Holiness. Did you have a good breakfast?"

The Pope said, "Not like in the old days," in a very weak voice. "I had a soft-boiled egg, toast and tea. Not too filling."

"How are you feeling?" inquired Vellini. The Pope gave a weak smile and said, "I've been better."

Vellini said, "We must talk, your Holiness. Cardinal Burns, Cardinal Salvemini and I have been discussing your health with Dr. Santos. Your infection needs more aggressive treatment. Your kidneys need the help of a dialysis machine. You need around-the-clock care. All of this cannot be done here, but can be accomplished in a hospital."

The Pope said, "What will happen to all the work going on in the Vatican? If I am not seen by the public in these trying times, the Church could suffer greatly. It would be better if I died today."

Vellini looked at his old friend and said, "Let's not talk about death, Holiness. We have a plan." He told the Pope about the look-alike, about the transplant, and said,

"With good care, Dr. Santos tells me you could be your old self in about two months."

The Pope looked at him and said, "Is it worth it?"

Vellini said, "Holiness, at the present, you are the balance between the left and right. If the College of Cardinals were to convene, I'm afraid there would be a real battle. We could go backwards to the time of the Reformation. In addition, it would be a sin if we let you die with a cure at hand."

After a long time the Pope said, "So be it. Proceed, but keep me advised."

Chapter 12

Father Ronald knocked, and then went into the Bishop's office. He walked to the desk and said, "Bishop, you have a special letter from Rome."

The Bishop said, "Open and read it."

When he was finished, Father Ronald said, "I wonder what this is all about. Why could they want a double for the Pope?"

The Bishop said, "I do not know, but after the assassination attempt, maybe it is some new security procedure."

The Bishop put the letter in his desk drawer and said, "Father, look through all the pictures we have of our people and see what you can find. Also, check the computer on background and education."

Ron said, "I will do it right away. The letter seems to say that they want this person as soon as possible."

Chapter 13

Father Stephan and Dick had finished dinner and were lingering over their tea. They had shared Peking duck and sweet and sour pork. During the dinner they had been discussing what they had found in the archives regarding the Society of Jesus.

Dick said, "When I was in town I stopped to see an old friend at his restaurant. He told me one of the local mob leaders wants to put a contract out on the Pope."

Father Stephan asked why.

Dick said, "Manny Salvador has the belief that the Church is persecuting him." Dick explained about the destruction of the cocaine factories and the refusal to grant him an annulment.

Father Stephan said, "He sounds like a real nut case."

Dick replied, "Yes, just enough of a nut that this could be true."

Father Stephan asked, "What are you going to do about it?"

Dick said, "I believe I will call Father Jason and see what happens."

Stephan looked at him and said, "If he does anything, that will tell you a lot about the little red shield on his sleeve. It still has meaning."

Dick answered, "Exactly."

Ronald had been working on the computer trying to find someone in the personnel files that fit the description in the letter from Rome. He started with those men who were the approximate age of the Pope and after about a half hour he came up with one. He checked the background and the education of the person he had found. Now, he thought, if this person looks anything like the Pope, we are in. He got up from his computer desk and walked down the hall to the Bishop's office. He knew that by habit the Bishop would still be there and working.

He knocked on the door, entered, and said, "Bishop, I think we may have a candidate. I don't know about the man's appearance, but his background fits to a tee. I did find an old picture, but nothing up-to-date."

The Bishop said, "Who is he?"

Father Ronald responded, "A professor at Yale Divinity School. His name is Father Stephan Zablonski."

The Bishop said, "Will you please contact him and see if it would be convenient for him to be here Monday morning at 10? We will pay his travel expenses. And, oh yes, by the way, do we happen to know anybody in the theatrical business who is good at makeup and can be trusted?"

Father Ron thought for a moment and then said, "Yes, I have an old friend I will contact. His name is Jim Banks."

Father Ron went back to his office and placed a call to Father Stephan at home. He left a message and relayed the Bishop's wishes. He then went through the Rolodex, found Jim Banks name and number and dialed.

A cheery voice answered the phone and said, "Hello, this is Jim."

Father Ron said, "Jim, this is Ron."

Jim said, "Great! It's been a long time, Ron. How are you doing?"

Father Ron answered, "Fine."

Teasingly Jim asked, "Are you still trying to save the world?"

Father Ron said, "No, I'm now working for the Bishop, shuffling more paper than saving souls." Both men laughed.

Jim said, "What can I do for you, Ron?"

Father Ron said, "Do you know anybody in the business who is expert in the art of makeup?"

In his teasing manner, Jim asked, "What do you want to do? Change your appearance and rob banks to raise money for the Church?"

Father Ron said, "No, something a little more serious than that."

Jim said, "Oh boy, how quickly we forget. Don't you remember how I started into this business when we were in school?"

Ron said, "That's right. You always had a makeup kit. I remember how you used to make up the kids in the neighborhood so they could go out and do Halloween tricks."

Jim said, "You are right. I'm your man. What can I do for you?"

Father Ron said, "I may need your expertise. Could you please be at the Bishop's office at 10:15 on Monday morning?"

Jim said, "Ron, I'd be happy to and I'll be glad to see you again."

Ron said, "Okay, I'll see you then."

Chapter 14

Wally walked into Manny's office and said hello to the secretary. She nodded toward the open door and said, "Go right in," and he did. Manny was on the phone. Wally seated himself at the comfortable chair in front of Manny's desk and waited until his phone call was finished.

Wally's expression suggested that he was not in agreement with the task that Manny had assigned to him. He looked into Manny's eyes and said, "Boss, if you really want to go through with this, I think I may have a man who will do the job. I have been in contact with some of our business associates in France and there may be a man who will take the contract."

Manny stiffened at Wally's apparent reluctance. However, he soon calmed down.

"Yes, I want to go through with this and you get me somebody to do it."

Wally said, "All right. Moe will drive me home, I will pack a few things and get a flight out tonight." Manny asked, "How are you set for money?" Wally said, "Okay, and I also have the company credit card, if needed. Nevertheless, boss, this might cost you some real money."

"I do not care how much it costs," responded Manny.

Wally said, "Okay then, I will take off." On the way out of the office he asked the secretary to make reservations on a flight to Paris for sometime that evening and to give him a call at his apartment. He walked down the hall of the office suite and stopped at a room used as a gathering place for various members of the organization. Moe was seated inside, reading a paper. Wally said, "Moe, you gotta drive me home and then out to the airport. Okay?" Moe said, "Yup."

There was only one word to describe Moe, and that was BIG. He sometimes served as a chauffeur, or bodyguard, but all around 'go-fer' for anybody in the organization.

Wally walked toward the exit with Moe lumbering after him. Three and a half hours later they seated Wally in the first class section of the flight to Paris. There were very few people in this part of the plane. He settled into his seat, fastened his seat belt, closed his eyes and waited for the plane to take off. He was deep in thought as the plane left the runway and headed into the sky. He thought to himself, "I wonder if Sam got my message to the proper people? In a way it's kind of funny. I put out a warning, yet I have to do what I have to do . . ." It wasn't long before he was fast asleep.

Chapter 15

After dinner, Dick accompanied Father Stephan home. As was his habit, Father Stephan said Mass at the little church two blocks away. He had asked Dick to be the lector and Dick had agreed. Dick went to the kitchen and was going to make coffee when he noticed Father's answering machine blinking. He called, "Steph, you have some messages on your machine."

Father Stephan came in, pressed the button, and listened to the message from Father Ron. Dick looked at Father Stephan and said,

"Have you been a bad boy, being summoned to the Bishop's office?"

Stephan said, "No, and I have no idea what he wants. My order as a special project has assigned me here and I really do not come under the Bishop's office. Nevertheless, we will find out tomorrow."

After they finished their coffee, they went into the living room. Dick said to Stephan, "Do you mind if I use your phone? I will give Father Jason a call and let him know what I found out from Sam."

Father Stephan said, "Good, we may find out more than one thing."

Dick looked in his little book, found the number and dialed Father Jason's office. Soon, Jason answered the phone and Dick said, "Hello there, this is Dick Rogers."

Father Jason said, "Good evening."

Dick said, "I hope I am not bothering you but I just wanted to tell you something. One of the people gave a very good friend, a man whom I trust, a message from the organized crime area. He told me that Manny Salvador, due to his frustration with the Catholic Church, was going to put a contract out on the Pope's life."

For a moment there was silence on the other end of the line, then Father Jason asked, "Why are you telling me?"

Dick said, "Because of that little red shield on the sleeve of your coat."

Father Jason said, "Oh, all right. I will pass the message along."

Dick said, "Thank you," and they hung up. Dick then looked at Father Stephan and said, "He told me he would take care of it, so our assumptions must be correct."

Father Stephan said, "Could be and he might be of much help."

Father Jason sat and looked at the wall for a long time. He studied the picture of the Pope that hung over his desk. Finally, he took a key from his pocket, opened the center desk drawer, and took out a black pocket notebook. Inside it were names, addresses and phone numbers of people all over the world. These were his contacts for information and for projects, whatever they might be. As he leafed through the book, he stopped at one page, put his finger on a name, picked up the phone, cradled it between his shoulder and ear, and punched out the number.

When the phone rang and the person on the other end identified himself, Jason said, "Who is number one? Who has the control in the crime families?"

The voice answered, telling him the necessary information. He closed the book, put it back in the desk drawer, and again locked it, and put the key in his pocket. Again he picked up the phone, and said, "I would like a ticket from New York to Rome." He gave his name and his credit card number and found that he could leave the next afternoon at 1:00. While he was drifting off to sleep, he thought about how he came to be in his present circumstances.

Father Jason Skinner had been connected with the Army for most of his life. His father came up through the ranks and retired as a full Colonel. As a youngster, Jason used to imitate the soldiers doing physical training. He loved to watch the Jeeps roll out on maneuvers in the vast expanse of the Army camp. Not only did he keep himself in good physical condition but he also was an excellent student and participated in ROTC at the schools on Army bases.

He graduated from high school and enlisted in the Army. Because of the ROTC training and a special officer's school, he made 2nd Lieutenant. They shipped him to Vietnam, and after only four weeks in the field, his company commander was killed, and Jason took over with the rank of 1st Lieutenant. He was a person who was destined to lead, and that's exactly what he did. He sent no one where he would not go himself. On more than one occasion, he took risks to save some of his men who might have been trapped or killed. He received the Silver Star twice and also a battlefield promotion to Captain. He volunteered and was accepted to go behind enemy lines to work with the mountain people. He enjoyed working with these people, as they lived off the land and were very much at home in the jungle. Out on patrol to harass the enemy, he was shot. A bullet entered his upper right arm and broke the bone in several pieces. Several of the mountain people took him to a place where he could be picked up by helicopter. He received some surgery but was sent back to an Army hospital in the United States where the bone was pieced together.

Jason's roommate during his time in the hospital introduced himself as Sam. He was a dark-haired, sun-tanned, cheery individual whose body was in a cast. His arms had been lifted to shoulder height and bent forward at the elbows so that his fingertips almost touched. There were braces from each elbow down to his side. He looked like a bird about ready to take off.

Jason asked Sam, "How did your injury happen?"

Sam answered, "I was in a helicopter. One of the VC had a ground-to-air missile and knocked us out of the sky. I was one of the lucky ones."

With that a nurse came into the room. She said, "Father Sam, are you ready for X-ray?"

Jason looked at his roommate and said, "*Father* Sam?"

Father Sam answered, "Yes, I'm a Jesuit priest."

Jason asked, "What were you doing in a helicopter?"

"Oh," said Sam, "I was going up to a patrol base to say Mass, talk to the men and share some of the gifts my home diocese had given me."

"Wasn't it a little odd to be up in the forward area?"

Father Sam answered, "No. Many of the clergy go up to be with the soldiers in the field. That's our job. If you want to take care of the flocks, you have to go where the flock is."

Sam made a deep impression on Jason. Over the next several weeks the two of them had long conversations, not only about life in general and the priesthood, but also about theology and faith. Jason had been born and raised Catholic. However, he had never been a devout practitioner.

The longer they talked, the more an idea formed in Jason's mind. About two weeks before they discharged him from the hospital he looked at Father Sam and said, "Sam, I think I may enter a seminary and study to become a priest."

Father Sam was delighted and suggested his old seminary. He added that Jason would make an excellent Jesuit. Jason did extremely well in his seminary work. He was enthusiastic about any project given to him. He studied long and hard. At his graduation they decided that the best spot for him to start would be to teach. The year after his first assignment, he was recruited by an older priest into the brotherhood of the red shield.

When Jason awoke, he finished his preparations and by the next afternoon, he boarded a plane in New York and was off on his journey to Rome.

Chapter 16

As Beau and Bob walked down the steps of the apartment building, Beau said, "You know, I do not think the mother or the kid had a full mainspring."

Bob said, "Yep, that apartment was something else, wasn't it? Very freaky."

Beau answered, "Weird is the word for it. Do you want to walk the couple of blocks to the mother's house or shall we drive?"

Bob said, "Let's walk, we need the exercise and besides we can build up an appetite for lunch."

They stood in front of 210 Fairview. Like the other buildings, it was rundown and needed a lot of paint and repair. They went into the vestibule and looked at the mailboxes. Beau pushed the button under the little sign, "Mrs. John O'Neill." A little voice answered, "Who is it?"

Bob said, "Policemen. May we come up to see you, please?"

When they heard the sound of the buzzer, they went into the hallway and up the stairs to Apartment 2B, which they had noted on the mailbox. They were about to knock on the door when it opened a slight crack. Bob could see the chain was still on. The woman behind the door asked for their identification. The men showed their cards and shields. She closed the door, took off the chain and opened it, saying, "Come in."

She was a small, frail-looking woman dressed in a neat, flowered housedress. As they looked around they were surprised. Everything was neat as a pin. The furniture was well worn, as was the rug. But everything was in its place and was clean. They entered the living room and she said, "Please be seated," and gestured toward the couch.

Bob said, "Mrs. O'Neill, I believe someone came here to advise you of the death of your grandson?"

She said, "Yes, yes . . . . terrible, wasn't it? But he was always getting into trouble and I really expected it someday. He was not a very pleasant boy."

"Did you see him often?"

"I did not see him often, just like I did not see his mother. They kept to themselves in their own little world. The only time I saw them was when they were in trouble or needed money."

Beau said, "Please tell us about your daughter."

"Well," said Mrs. O'Neill, "she went to a parochial grammar school and enjoyed it very much. She liked working with the nuns. At one time all she talked about was becoming a nun and I thought that might be good. Then she went to a public high school, and after a couple of years, she started to change. She wore funny clothes. She went out more, but every once in awhile she would say she still wanted to be a nun. She was invited to a party. I didn't know any of the kids she was going with. She did not come home until late and then I smelled alcohol on her breath. I don't know, maybe I was too strict or not strict enough. About a month and a half later she said she thought she was pregnant. I took her to the doctor and sure enough, she was. That was about the time my husband died, so I had to go to work and take care of her and myself throughout the pregnancy. All she could talk about was how this was going to kill any hopes she had of becoming a nun. When the baby was several months old, she got a job as a typist. After a few months, she moved into her own apartment. She wanted her independence, but still kept blaming that child for interfering with her life. I really don't think she ever loved him."

Bob said,"What kind of a boy was he?"

"Well, the usual type of boy in grammar school, but as soon as he got to high school he skipped classes. He was caught smoking by the principal, sent home, and he was always getting into trouble. I think he was arrested for stealing something, I can't remember. But I did not have much contact with either of them. It seemed to me that both of them, as the years passed, sort of went downhill. I was in her apartment once, and she had a shrine in her living room. It seemed to be out of proportion, not at all what a normal person would do. And her son was involved in all kinds of crazy things. He collected knives; he got into one jam after another. I haven't seen either of them for over four years, and now the city will have to bury him, because I don't have the money to do so. I really don't know if I will go to the funeral or not. That's how broken-hearted I am."

Beau said, "Ma'am, you can help kids when they're small, but you don't have to blame yourself for anything that happened, because it is surely not your fault."

Mrs. O'Neill said, "Thank you. You're very understanding."

Bob looked at Mrs. O'Neill and said, "Well, we thank you very much for filling us in. We'll be going now."

Mrs. O'Neill responded, "I'm sorry I couldn't be of more help."

Beau said, "But you have helped, ma'am. Thank you!"

They got up and walked to the door. She closed it quietly behind them. As they walked down the hall, Beau said, "I feel sorry for the old lady."

Bob said, "So do I."

When they were out on the street again, Bob said, "You know, I think I'm going to call the departmental shrink and see if I can get an appointment. I'll lay this out for her to see what she thinks."

Beau said, "Good idea. Are you going to do it now?"

Bob said, "Yes."

They stopped in a drugstore, got a cup of coffee, and Bob made his call to the office of the police psychiatrist. It just so happened that she had the next hour free.

On the door, painted on the glass, was *Dr. Karen Billings*. Beau and Bob walked in. The secretary knew them both and said, "You can go right in. The doctor is waiting for you."

They entered the inner office, and Dr. Karen, as they called her, motioned for them to be seated. Beau explained about the knifing of the nun and the attack on the other nun. He explained in detail what they had found in the apartment and also what O'Neill's grandmother had told them.

Karen thought for quite a long while then said, "Well, not being able to talk with the individual, I'll make some assumptions. If what you tell me is true about the mother in her final years always dressing in black and having a habit in her closet and belittling her son constantly for frustrating her plans that she had as a teenager, I would say John O'Neill had a hatred not only for his mother, but also for that symbol of being a nun. This hate could have built to a point where he needed to destroy it. By killing the nun, in reality, he was killing his own mother. He made the attacks in the blackness of pre-dawn, which sort of fits the picture. I don't believe he would have done anything like that in the daylight. If he had not been stopped this time, he would have gone on and on. I don't believe a nun in the city would have been safe as long as she wore black. There's a good possibility he may have extended beyond that line and killed anyone he knew was a nun."

"So what you're saying is, he was a real sick-o?"

"Well," Karen said, "that's not a very good technical term you're using. Again, I didn't know the individual, nor did I work with him, but I would have said, either schizophrenic or psychotic. Both are quite severe."

Bob said, "Thanks a lot, doc, for your time. I think this will help us out."

They shook hands and the detectives left.

Chapter 17

At two minutes of ten, Father Stephan entered the anteroom of the Bishop's office. A young priest was standing over the Secretary's desk with a sheaf of papers in his hand. He was explaining something to her. He turned at the sound of the door opening, put the papers on the desk, and extended his right hand and said, "Hi. I am Father Ron."

Father Stephan shook his hand and said, "I am Father Stephan."

Father Ron said, "The Bishop's waiting. Let's go right in."

As they entered the Bishop's office, the Bishop stood up and walked toward the two priests. He extended his hand to Father Stephan. Father Stephan was about to kneel and kiss the Bishop's ring. The Bishop said, "No, no, no." As they stood there, the Bishop looked Father Stephan over from head to foot, concentrating on the features of his face.

"Father, please bear with me. Don't think I have lost my mind. Would you step over here, please?".

He guided Father Stephan to a wall where hung the picture of the Pope and placed him facing into the room. He stood back. He and Father Ron looked at the picture and then at Father Stephan. He shook his head and said, "Yes, I think we will be all right."

The Bishop then motioned Father Stephan to take one of the comfortable chairs in front of his desk. He sat facing Father Stephan and said, "I understand you are a linguist."

Father Stephan said, "Yes, I think you could say that."

The Bishop asked,"How many languages do you speak?"

"Six, but I am studying a seventh—Chinese."

The Bishop said, "Good, very good. I understand you are doing a book on church history."

Father Stephan said, "Yes, I am. That is what I teach, besides languages, at the University."

The Bishop said, "Excellent. Father, would you humor me and allow us to have your appearance changed somewhat?"

Father Stephan said, "Well, if there is a good reason for it I will not object."

The Bishop then motioned to Father Ron to get the letter. Father Ron handed the letter to Father Stephan and he slowly read it. When he was finished, he looked questioningly at the Bishop and said, "I do not understand."

The Bishop said, "Apparently Rome would like to have someone who looks similar to the Pope. Also, having a background in language and an understanding of church hierarchy and history, would qualify you. Would you be willing to go to Rome?"

Father Stephan said, "If it's necessary and important to them, surely."

The Bishop turned to Father Ron and said, "Ron, will you call Rome and talk with the Cardinal. Tell him we think we have found what he needs. Also, you might explain that I do not think we can have a person with a very close resemblance to the Pope walking in the front door of the Vatican. So we will have your friend work on Father Stephan and then we might have to come up with some sort of disguise that he can wear."

Father Ron was about to answer when the intercom rang. He picked it up and said, "Will you show him in, please," and replaced the phone. He said to the Bishop,

"Jim Banks, the make-up specialist, is here." Father Ron walked to the door, opened it and said, "Come on in, Jim," shook his hand, took him over to the Bishop and Father Stephan and introduced him. Both men stood. Jim knelt and kissed the Bishop's ring, then shook hands with Father Stephan.

He turned to the Bishop and said, "What can I do for you?"

The Bishop had Father Stephan walk over and stand next to the picture of the Pope. He looked at Jim and said, "Do you see a strong resemblance?"

Jim said, "Yes, very strong!"

"Do you think a hair cut and styling would make it even better?"

Jim replied, "Yes, it would."

The Bishop looked at Jim and said, "I understand you're a trustworthy man. All of this has to be in strictest confidence. I would like to have you supervise whatever has to be done to make Father Stephan look as much like the Pope as possible."

Jim said, "That will be no problem with his normal features."

Then the Bishop added, "But afterwards, we need to put him in some sort of disguise. We cannot have him going around looking like the Pope. Too many questions would be asked. We need some sort of disguise."

Jim said, "Again, no problem. We can blacken his hair with a coloring agent. Then all he will need is soap and water to wash it out, and he will have his gray hair again. We could give him horn-rimmed glasses that would have plain glass in them. They would change his appearance. And maybe even a false moustache."

The Bishop said, "That sounds very good. Could this last 24 to 36 hours?"

Jim said, "No problem. We do it all the time. When can we do this?" Jim asked Father Ron.

"Today, if you wish."

Jim said, "That will be very good. Here is my card with the address. What do you say if I meet you here about two. I have a luncheon meeting which should be short."

Looking at Father Stephan he said, "Father, do you have a pair of slacks and a sports shirt?"

Father Stephan said, "Yes, casual wear that I use around the house."

Jim said, "The wilder the sports shirt, the better. We do not want you looking like a priest and if anybody asks, you're a character actor and you've been on several TV shows, maybe westerns. What I am planning to do is produce a new mystery, a murder mystery, made for TV only and the Pope is going to help solve the mystery. So that is what you are going to do. You are going to be an actor in this TV mystery. Can you handle that, Father Stephan?"

Father Stephan said, "I think I can do it without really lying. I used to do some acting, but that was a long time ago, so I will put it in the past."

The Bishop extended his hand and said, "Thank you very much, Jim. Father Stephan will be there with Ron at 2 o'clock."

Father Stephan said, "I have a friend waiting for me downstairs. He can be trusted completely. Is it all right if I bring him along? We planned originally to stop here and then return to the Monastery to get back to our work."

Jim said, "That is fine with me."

The Bishop said, "Yes, it will be all right, as long as he can be trusted."

Father Stephan said, "I would trust him with my life."

Jim left and the three clergymen were alone together. The Bishop said, "I do not know what this is all about but I thank you, Father, for being so cooperative."

Father Stephan looked very serious and said to the Bishop, "I hope it does not have anything to do with a bit of news that I have heard."

The Bishop said, "What's that?"

Father Stephan said, "One of the local mobsters would like to have the Pope assassinated."

The Bishop gasped, "Oh, my Lord. I hope it does not have anything to do with that, either."

Father Ron asked, "What are we going to do about that news?"

Father Stephan said, "My friend, who is downstairs, has many contacts with security people. The word has already been passed, so I imagine that Rome is aware. That is all we can do at the present time." Then he said, "Well, I had better be going. I will get my friend, we'll have lunch, and then go over to see Jim."

Father Ron said, "Do you mind if I come with you?"
Father Stephan said, "No."

The Bishop extended his hand and put his left hand on Father Stephan's shoulder and said, "Thank you very much."

Ron and Stephan left. When they got downstairs, Stephan looked at Dick and smiled and said, "Richard, our plans have been somewhat changed. You and I are going to embark on an adventure. I hope you are equipped for it."

Chapter 18

Seated in a very quiet corner of the restaurant as Dick and the two priests ate, Father Stephan explained to Dick what had happened. Dick looked at Father Stephan and said, "Remember what I said to you when you were sitting in the living room the other night, and I looked at the picture of the Pope over your fireplace?"

Father Stephan said, "Yes. Who knows, maybe you caused this," and chuckled.

"You know Steph, I have been doing some serious thinking about what I heard from my friend. I think I will go over to Europe myself and see if I can see an old friend who probably could give me some good information to pass on.".

Father Stephan said, "That sounds like a good idea. Why don't you fly over to Rome, and remember that delightful little hotel we stayed at, let's see, it was two years ago, wasn't it?"

Dick said, "Yes, I liked that place. Nevertheless, I will stick with you until all the changes are made. I do not want you to go home and scare the cat."

Father Stephan said to Ron, "How soon do you think they will want me over there?"

Ron said, "I really do not know, but when I sent the telegram, I asked them. When I hear from them, I will contact you."

Having gone home and changed, Father Stephan and the other two men were on time for their appointment with Jim. As they walked into his office, Jim looked up and said,

"Boy, that is a wild shirt!"

Father Stephan said, "First time I have ever worn it."

Jim stood up from his desk, picked up a file folder and said, "Come on, let's go get the locks cut off."

They walked down the hall and into a room. In the center was a chair, not unlike a barber's chair, one that could be raised and lowered.

"This is where we perform the magic on people's faces and heads."

In the corner was a young man with very dark hair and a thin line moustache. Jim said,

"Tony, if you can perform a miracle, this is going to be my newest star in a mystery. Father Ron is a friend of mine who wants to see the miracles we work here."

Tony looked around and said, "Glad to know you both. What do you want me to do, Jim?"

Jim produced an 8 1/2" colored photograph of the Pope from his file folder and he said,

"I want you to give him a haircut just like this. Make him look as much like this picture as possible."

Tony asked, "What are you going to do, make a documentary on the Vatican?"

Jim said, "Nope. The Pope is going to solve a murder mystery for me."

Tony said, "You're kidding!"

Jim said, "Look, if Miss Marple can do it for Agatha Christie, the Pope can do it for me!"

Tony had Father Stephan sit in the chair and draped a cloth around his shoulders. He set the picture up on a table next to the chair. He started snipping away and said, "You know that is a wild shirt you have on."

Father Stephan said, "Yes, it was a birthday present."

Tony asked, "What have you been doing in the profession?"

Father Stephan thought for a moment and said, "Character acting." This really was not a lie because many of his students looked upon him as a character. He continued, "I am glad I ran into Jim. It is the first lead part I have ever had. You had better do a good job."

Tony said, "Don't worry. You are going to be great!" After about 45 minutes with little scissor snips here and there, filling the time, Tony said, "What do you think, Jim?" He held up the picture about six inches from Father Stephan's head.

Jim said, "That is marvelous!"

Father Ron looked on in amazement and said, "If you walked into the room and I did not know who you were, I'd probably die of a heart attack. The resemblance is amazing. Thank you, Tony, you have done a great job!"

Tony said, "You're welcome. Hey, by the way," addressing himself to Father Stephan, "I hope you do well and solve the murder mystery."

Father Stephan said, "Thank you, so do I."

Jim took the two priests down the hall. He unlocked the door, opened it, and had them enter, and he followed. He flicked on a light switch and there, along one wall was a big mirror with lights all around it. In front was a counter top with bottles, tubes, brushes and all kinds of paraphernalia. Jim had Father Stephan sit in a chair facing the mirror. The chair was much like the one in Tony's room.

Jim said, "Please sit, Father," and Stephan did. Jim said, "Now, for another re-creation." He tilted the chair back, draped a cloth around Father Stephan's neck so that it covered him completely, went to the counter, got a jar and a stiff little brush. He dipped the brush into the jar and applied the gel to Father Stephan's hair. After a few minutes, the hair turned black. With a comb and brush, Jim styled the hair differently than it had been. Next he went to the cabinet and after searching for a minute, came out and placed a pair of black rimmed glasses on Father Stephan's face. Father Stephan looked at himself and could not believe the sight. He was another person. Jim said,

"Ron, what do you think?"

Ron said, "What a difference. Nobody would know him."

Jim said, "I don't think we are going to use a beard or moustache. That could prove a problem. If I understand you correctly, you will be taking a couple of flights and be in extremely warm weather. I have the adhesive that would hold the moustache, but I do not think we will need it. Instead, I am going to give you something else."

Again he walked to the cabinet and looked through several small boxes. He turned and brought out two paper-covered objects. He had Father Stephan lean back further in the chair, tore open the packages and said, "Father, open your mouth, please." When Father Stephan did, Jim put two small pads in his mouth between his teeth and cheeks.

"There, I think that might be better. This will give you the appearance of having gained ten pounds as far as your face is concerned and if you are really careful, they will stay in place and you can even eat with them in your mouth."

When Father Stephan looked at himself in the mirror, he was even more amazed. He looked at Jim and said, "You know if you did this to some person who had been drinking a lot and he woke up the next morning and looked in the mirror, he would not know who he was."

Jim said, "That's a good idea. I think I will try it out on a few friends of mine."

Jim looked at Ron and said, "There you go. It's all set. I will give you a bottle of this stuff in case you have to re-dye your hair. Maybe you won't need it but you had better take it with you and be prepared. The pads will last, so there is no problem with them or with the glasses."

He turned to Father Stephan and said, "I want to try an experiment, if you would, Father." Walking to a cabinet along the wall, he opened the doors, looked and took out a shirt saying, "Here, Father, take off your shirt and put this one on. It looks as if it might match your trousers."

Father Stephan did as he was told, standing there in the room with tan slacks and a tan shirt to match.

Jim said, "Come on, let's give our talent a test," and they walked back down the hall to Tony's room. As they did, they stopped and Jim said, "Thanks again, Tony. That was a great job you did." Father Ron said, "Yes, it was very instructive. I want to thank you again too."

Tony said, "Well, thank you, thank you. It was great showing off. Oh, where did the other guy go to," looking straight at Father Stephan?

Jim said, "Oh, he had to leave early. Thanks again, Tony. Take care."

Chapter 19

At the entrance to the building, Jim shook hands with Dick and Father Stephan. The two men thanked Jim for all of his help and assistance. Jim said, "Good luck on your venture!"

They bade goodbye and walked down to their car. Father Stephan was going to drop Dick off at his apartment building. He had decided to pack, get his passport, and make some telephone calls to some old associates from his Army Intelligence days. As he got out of the car he said, "Well, Steph, take care of yourself. I will see you over in Rome."

Father Stephan said, "I do not know where this is going to lead, but it should prove interesting. Take care, Dick," and Father Stephan drove away.

It was too late to call any of his old contacts in Europe so Dick went up to his apartment, packed and made sure he had his passport and enough money.

The next morning, he called the hotel in Rome and made reservations for two. One room was in his name. The other was in the name of Stephan Zablonski. He made three other calls. On the third one, he had success and was able to secure information on the man he was seeking. He took a cab to the airport and boarded the Air Italia plane bound for Rome. About 45 minutes later the plane took off. As they soared to 35,000 feet, Dick looked out of the window and could see the reflection of the sun on the clouds. The beautiful white, billowy clouds were tinged with red, yellow and orange, as if an artist had painted a gigantic picture. Watching the colorful clouds with the black background of night,

Dick was awed. His thoughts turned to the task ahead and the man he was going to see.

He had known Nicolai Andropov since the early days in Army Intelligence. They had assigned Dick to the Embassy as Military Attaché. Nicolai, or Nicky, as he called him, had the same job at his embassy. They first met at an embassy party and entered into a conversation, each sizing the other up. Dick, in intelligence, and Nicky, as an agent of the KGB, both held the rank of Captain.

As time passed, they engaged in a game of one-up-manship. First Dick would ferret out some plot or plan that the Russians had to obtain information from the Allies. Then Nicky would do the same. Over time, they grew to have great respect for one another.

About a year and a half after they first met, Dick got a call from Nicky asking him to join him for dinner at a small restaurant near checkpoint Charlie. Dick said he would. Dick had dined there several times and found that certain of the German dishes were excellent.

They were seated at a table near the front window so they could look out. Both were dressed in civilian clothes. After they had ordered, Nicky asked, "Have you heard about a small gang that is operating out of the area?"

Dick said, "I have had some information, but nothing really concrete."

Nicky said in a hushed voice, "Well, it seems to be made up of some Americans, Germans, and amazingly, several Russians. They not only deal in black market merchandise on both sides of the border, but if you have the money, they will eliminate anybody that you wish."

Dick said, "That could be bad for both sides."

Nicky said, "Exactly. Would you want to work together on this?"

Dick said, "Yes, if we play it across the board and both are honest with one another."

Nicky said, "Nothing else but!" He passed Dick a card with a telephone number on it, saying, "This is my private line."

Dick also gave Nicky a phone number. They did not wish to go through their office phones as they probably were tapped. By virtue of some contacts that Dick had on the street, he learned that this group met, on occasion, in a restaurant near the one where he and Nicky were dining. Usually after dark, Dick would park almost across the street from the entrance to the restaurant. He used a civilian car that belonged to the Army. One evening he got lucky. As he was sitting in his car, he recognized one of the men from the gang. One of his informants had given a description to him. He picked up his camera and started snapping pictures. The camera used infrared film, and Dick had preset the distance when he first arrived.

He put the camera back on the seat. Next to it was an automatic pistol. Sitting there, slouched behind the wheel, he noticed a figure walking toward the group. When the figure reached the bright light up over the door of the restaurant, he said to himself, "My God, it is Nicky!" As he watched, apparently one of the men recognized Nicolai, pulled out a knife and held his arm straight out with the point about a foot away from Nicky's throat. The man holding the knife said in a voice, loud enough for Dick to hear,

"This is the pig—KGB—that has been spying on us. I think it is time to butcher the pig."

Dick grabbed hold of the automatic, quietly opened his door and the passenger side door, got out, and crouched in the shadow of the door and yelled in a loud voice,

"Nicky, over here!"

The yell startled the man with the knife and he glanced toward the opposite side of the street. This gave Nicky a chance. He balanced himself firmly on one foot and with the other, kicked the man as hard as he could in the crotch. The man dropped the knife immediately, clutched himself, and dropped to his knees moaning. Nicky ran quickly to the car. As he did, Dick started to spray the brick building with bullets just over the heads of the rest of the men. They all dropped to the sidewalk, pinned down and unable to return fire. Nicky jumped into the car as did Dick, started it, and sped off. When they were about a half block away, Nicky looked at Dick and said, "I owe you one," and thanked him. He continued, "You know the guy with the knife really did not know how to use it. He was not standing correctly. He should have had one foot in front of the other. If he had, I would not have done what I did to him."

* * *

A hand on his shoulder brought Dick out of his deep thoughts. It was the flight attendant. She asked whether he wanted coffee or a snack and he said yes. He straightened up his reclining seat and pulled out the tray in front of him. When he was served, he enjoyed a delicious cheese croissant with his coffee. He finished the last bit of coffee and again put his seat back and looked out the window. The thoughts whirled around in his mind, and he remembered one time when he had to go over to East Berlin.

His papers, although forged, were perfect. He was going over on the pretense of visiting family. However, his real purpose was to pick up a roll of film from one of his agents. He strolled slowly away from the checkpoint and walked about eight blocks into what was a very drab and gloomy looking part of the city. He met his contact in an alleyway. The man was German and spoke with a very heavy accent. He was pushing a bicycle. As he approached Dick, he leaned the bicycle toward Dick and Dick grasped the handlebars. The man fumbled in his pocket and pulled out a small package. He handed this to Dick, who put it in his pocket. Just then a voice rang out that they should stop. A police officer approached them. The man, without hesitation, drew a revolver from his pocket and shot in the direction of the voice. Dick, still grasping the handlebars of the bicycle, moved out toward the street. When he realized what he was doing, he jumped on the bike and started pedaling toward the checkpoint. He was about a half block away. Dick approached the black car. He could see that an officer was sitting behind the wheel. When he was abreast of the car, a voice said,

"Come on, Dick, I will give you a ride."

Dick thought, "My God, it is Nicky!"

He leaned the bike against the wall, ran over to the passenger side and got in. Nicky started the car and they drove toward the checkpoint. Nicky was in the full-dress uniform of a Colonel. Dick said,

"What did you do, get promoted?"

Nicky said, "No, but I have the right papers and that is all they need to know."

When they got to the checkpoint, Nicky showed his papers to the guard on duty. The man snapped to attention and had the barrier raised. The two men drove back into the western zone. Nicky said,

"What happened? I heard a shot. Did something go wrong?"

Dick said, "Yup, we hired the wrong man, I guess."

Nicky said, "Oh well, you win some, you lose some."

* * *

Dick was very comfortable lying back in the seat on the plane. He could hear the drone of the engine and wondered what was below him on the black Atlantic. He fell into a deep sleep and slept all the way to Rome.

Dick had no trouble going through customs or getting his bags. He took a cab to the hotel and checked in. There were no messages, so, therefore, he thought, nothing new on Stephan. He went up to his room, took a shower, and went down to the restaurant to eat. He had planned to spend the rest of the day taking life easy and resting to get over his jet lag. He knew the next day he would be going to Berlin and maybe he would see Nicky.

The next morning, Dick arose early and had a good breakfast downstairs in the hotel restaurant. Back in his room, he packed an overnight bag that he had purchased in a store near the hotel. He then took a cab to the airport and got his ticket to Berlin.

Chapter 20

Cardinal Vellini was sitting at his desk reviewing correspondence and reports. His efficient secretary had sorted through all the papers and made individual piles according to subject matter. As he read a document, he would make notes on the paper or transfer it to someone else for some action. Since the Pope's illness, all the work had fallen on his shoulders. They put any important decisions that were the Pope's prerogatives on a separate pile. However, they acknowledged everything. In answer to a knock on the door, he said, "Come in," and a young priest entered the room. The Cardinal gestured to one of the two easy chairs that were off to the side of the desk, as he finished making a note on a piece of paper. When he was through, he stood, looked at the young man and said, "Would you like coffee?"

The young priest said, "Yes, Eminence, that would be enjoyable."

The Cardinal walked to a table that was in front of the window overlooking the big square of the Vatican. He brought a tray with coffee, cream, sugar and spoons on it and placed it on the table between them. He had ordered the coffee in anticipation of the young man's visit. Cardinal Vellini thought offering coffee would be one way of diminishing the man's nervousness. He thought back to when he was first ordained a priest and met a Bishop for the first time. He had been so nervous! Cardinal Vellini poured two cups of coffee.

"Would you like cream and sugar," asked the Cardinal?

"Thank you, no, Eminence."

The Cardinal said, "Ah, I enjoy my coffee black, also." He passed the cup to the young man and continued, "Tell me, Father O'Connor, where is your home?"

Father O'Connor said, "Outside the city of Dublin. I was born and raised there."

The Cardinal asked, "What did your father do?"

The young priest said, "My Dad was a machinist who worked in a mill."

"Your Mother, did she work also," asked the Cardinal?

"No, she was too busy taking care of all the children."

"How many were there," asked the Cardinal?

He said, "Six of us," in answer to the Cardinal's question. "She did work as a volunteer for our church, though."

"Tell me, Father, what made you want to become a priest?"

The young man thought for a moment and said, "Well, I found the Bible very interesting, and I read many books that our parish priest lent me about the church and the saints."

"Did you have a favorite?"

The young man smiled and said, "Yes, St. Francis of Assisi."

The Cardinal said, "Well, you are a long way from feeding the animals and birds."

The young man smiled in return and said, "Yes, but we do have pigeons all around the place and every once in awhile I feed them."

The Cardinal looked at the young man and said, "Father, you probably are very curious as to your sessions with Dr. Santos. Before I go any farther, I would like your sacred promise that anything said in this room from now on will stay between us."

Father O'Connor said, "Yes, Eminence, I promise that."

The Cardinal stood up, walked across the room, turned and said, "What I am about to tell you is very serious. First I would like to ask you a question. If it were in your power, how far would you go to maintain the stability of the Church?"

The young man also turned serious and said, "Eminence, if necessary, I would give my life."

The Cardinal looked at him, gave a gentle smile and said, "No one would ask you to do that. You probably know that we have several factions in the Church. One is ultra-liberal, the other, ultra-conservative. Each one is vying to get its ideas through." He continued, "We are living in a world that is changing faster than most of us can comprehend. Doing business as we have always done is being overshadowed by change throughout the world, but we must attend to the basic precept of morality. This can never be changed. The Holy Father has been a balance wheel between the two factions. Now I come to the part where you must never utter a word. The Holy Father is gravely ill. His kidneys are failing and he is fighting an infection. What the Pope needs is a kidney transplant."

Father O'Connor rose from his seat, walked toward the Cardinal and said, "Eminence, if I may . . ."

O'Connor continued, "I think what you are about to say is that I am a prime candidate for such a donation, is that not correct?"

The Cardinal responded, "Yes, but I want you to think long and hard about this decision."

Father O'Connor looked into the Cardinal's eyes and said, "Eminence, I have dedicated my life to the Church. There are those around the world that put their lives in jeopardy every day. There are so many who have died for the faith. I do not think giving one kidney is that important."

The Cardinal said, "You must be sure, my son, you must be sure."

Father O'Connor said, "Eminence, I am. I truly am. I would like to have your blessing."

He knelt, and the Cardinal blessed him. The Cardinal extended his hand as Father O'Connor rose to his feet. The Cardinal grasped his hand with a firm grip and said, "Thank you, my son, on behalf of the Church and His Holiness. I think now you had better go and see Dr. Santos. He may want to check you over and give you some instructions. Also, he can fill you in on some of the details."

Father O'Connor said, "Thank you, Eminence," turned and left the room.

Chapter 21

After landing in Paris, Wally had his bag and passport checked through customs. His passport read "Walter Monroe". However, this was not his real last name.

One afternoon, when Wally was 16, he and two friends were on the sidewalk in front of a store pitching pennies when they noticed a cop about a half block away. They scrambled, picked up the pennies and sat on the windowsill. As the cop approached, he walked up to Wally and said, "Son, what is your name?"

Wally stood up and gazed up and down the street. His eyes focused on the sign above a muffler repair shop halfway down the street. He looked at the cop and said,

"Monroe. Walter Monroe."

The cop said to him, "Well, that is an honest sounding name, but you should not be pitching pennies on the street." Wally decided right then if he were going to do anything that was against the law or cast doubt on his character he would make sure that no one saw him.

Wally's parents both worked and did not get home until six o'clock in the evening. This gave Wally several hours after school to roam the street with his friends. He did well in school, had above average grades, but his street roaming led to mischievous behavior. One of the favorite tricks of the three boys was to walk into a store and see which one could come out with the best prize without being caught. They did quite well with their thievery and took ever more valuable items. Wally was the best of the trio in stealing. One day when they were looking into the window of a jewelry store, Wally noticed on the counter not too far from the door a card displaying several wristwatches. He told the other two boys to go into the store and after a while start some sort of a commotion. The boys went in and walked to the back. Wally followed and stood admiring the watches. The clerk behind the counter paid almost no attention to Wally. Suddenly the boys in the back of the store started a fight and the clerk ran to stop them. Wally grabbed the card, put it under his jacket and slipped out of the store. He ran a couple of blocks down the street and sat on the steps of a brownstone. When the other two boys arrived, Wally divided the spoils of their latest adventure. Each of them then sold the watches.

Thievery was not limited to the local stores. When they could get out at night, they often stole batteries and radios out of cars. They then graduated to taking the wheels off the cars. These auto parts Wally sold to a local salvage yard. It was there that he met Manny Salvador. Manny was several years older than he and was the manager of the yard.

It got to a point where Manny told Wally what kind of automobile part he wanted and Wally would get several of his friends and deliver. Over time the friendship between Wally and Manny grew. When Wally graduated from high school, Manny gave him a job. The stolen parts business became so brisk that Wally decided not to fool with pieces. He would have his people steal the whole car. After instructions, any of his men, with the proper tools, could break into a locked car and drive it away within thirty seconds. They would drive the cars into a large building at the salvage yard. When the car was driven into the building, a group of men started to dismantle it. They removed identifying marks and serial numbers. They stamped new numbers on engines. They dipped doors, fenders and hoods in a vat of liquid. They were completely cleaned. After they were dried, they gave them a coat of paint that looked like a primer. As these pieces were hanging from racks, they looked like they had just shipped them in from the manufacturer. As they received orders from the various repair shops owned by the organization throughout the city, the pieces were loaded into a truck and shipped. They trucked the rest of the useful parts to a large warehouse south of the city. They put into the crusher and immediately demolished anything that could not be used. No traces of the stolen cars were ever found. Sometimes they had orders from foreign countries for special makes and models of automobiles. When they brought in one of these, it was placed in a large metal container. When the container was full for a certain country, it was picked up by a crane, loaded on a truck and taken to the docks where they put it on a ship for its final destination.

Although this was a very lucrative operation, Wally did not like it as it was too risky. They kept the cars around too long. Finally, Manny agreed and they ceased doing this type of business.

The salvage yard went so well that Manny's father moved him up to the front office, and Manny took Wally with him. Wally was a little concerned that his situation would change and he told Manny that he would never personally kill anyone. He stated that he had no compunction about setting somebody up, but he, personally, would never pull a trigger. Manny agreed to this, and they never asked Wally to get rid of anyone. Manny, on the other hand, had no qualms about pulling the trigger or using a knife or even an automobile as the weapon of destruction. Several times Wally was with Manny as Manny drove a car that hit someone, leaving the scene at high speed. A couple of times Wally arranged to obtain men to get rid of someone who was trying to muscle in on their territory. He became very good at getting things done or fixed.

Wally found that Tony, Manny's brother, was quite different. He was not as excitable and was probably more intelligent. Tony, essentially, oversaw the accounting procedures and worked mainly with the legitimate businesses. He negotiated with the other businessmen of the town with much ease. Wally also learned very quickly not to cross Tony. He never got violent, and anytime he was angry he spoke in a quiet voice. Nevertheless, Wally knew that Tony could be very dangerous.

Manny's father died, and Manny became number one. He made Wally his right-hand man. Because of this, Wally now found himself in Paris.

After a tiring trip of not sleeping too well, Wally decided to check into a hotel. At the check-in counter he made a reservation for a flight to Marseilles where a rental car would be waiting for him. He slept most of the day, got up, went downstairs to the restaurant and had a good meal. He then got a cab and because he had never been in Paris before, he went to see the sights. The cabby spoke English and drove him around the city and pointed out the landmarks. After about four hours, he asked the cabby to take him back to the hotel. Wally paid him, gave him a tip, and then returned to the restaurant. He had another good meal and later sat at the bar and had several drinks before heading to his room.

Early the next morning, he arose, showered, packed up his bag and went downstairs. He checked out and got a cab to take him to the airport. His flight to Marseilles was uneventful and very pleasant. Landing at Marseilles, he checked in with the car rental agency and started traveling west on the coast highway toward Narvonne. His destination was a small fishing village just west of the city. It was warm, bright and very pleasant. Sea breezes kept the air temperature at a comfortable level. Wally thought this would be a beautiful place to live, very warm, picturesque, then he said, "No, nothing here for me to do to keep life interesting."

After several hours of driving, he came to the village he was seeking. The place was quite a bit larger than he had imagined. It had been described to him as a small fishing village but it was a good deal more than that. He pulled up and parked in front of a white, two-story building with a veranda across the front. Up over the top was a sign, "White's Inn, Proprietor, Harry White." He thought it was odd that the sign was in English but then he turned his attention to the other buildings. They were a contrast in style and appearance. Some buildings were painted; others were weather-beaten from the sea, wind and sand. All were neat and clean. None of them looked as if they had been neglected. Across the street, about a quarter of a mile away, was the seashore. Extending into the water were two piers. Tied to these were several fishing boats, which were being unloaded. Scattered throughout the bay were buoys bobbing in the water. To some of these were tied other boats. On the beach, turned upside down, were smaller boats, and hanging from poles, there were fishnets drying in the sun.

Wally walked across the street and onto one of the wharves so that he could better see what was happening. The men on the first boat were off-loading fish. They would place them in a large plastic tub. Each layer of fish was then covered with ice. The ice was the consistency of the snow cones that Wally had enjoyed as a young boy. When a tub was full, they put it into the back of a truck, which appeared to him to be refrigerated. He thought, "Good Lord, this is a hard working bunch. They are up half the night trying to catch fish in nets, then putting them aboard the ship, and finally pulling into the wharf to unload their catch."

His interest turned to a machine on the deck. It seemed a marvel to him. The little engine chugged away and occasionally a man pulled a handle. Through a chute at the end would pour the granulated ice. He smiled and said, "Boy, a big snow cone maker!"

The men on the boat were quite jovial. They smiled and nodded to him, and he took this as a welcome. Although no one spoke, he thought probably, they would have difficulty in communicating because of the language barrier.

After about a half hour, Wally waved, turned and walked to the White building. Again he looked at the sign. His instructions were to come to this village and stop at the Cafe Blanc. Wally thought Blanc in French was White, so this must be the place.

He went back across the street, up the steps to the veranda and turned to look again out toward the sea. He thought it would be a very relaxing place to sit, rock, and watch the world.

Wally entered the building through the big double doors and found himself in a large room. To the left was a medium size bar and on the shelves behind were rows and rows of different colored bottles. In the main room itself, tables were scattered about. Each table was covered with a red and white-checkered tablecloth. On the center of each table, besides the condiments, was a lamp. The base of each was made from a different, extremely large shell. On the sidewall was a large blackboard, and neatly printed, was the menu of the day.

Behind the bar was a dark-haired man, graying at the temples. He seemed to be in good physical condition and stood erect in a military fashion. Wally walked over to the bar and said, "Bon jour."

The man responded, "Hi. I am Harry White."

This surprised Wally. Harry smiled and said, "You look like you are an American."

Wally said, "I am."

Harry said, "What can I do for you?"

Wally said, "First some conversation and then maybe some food."

Harry said, "Okay, what do you want to know?"

Wally said, "I am told that I can find a man here by the name of Rene, if I ask for him. Do you know him?"

Harry said, "No, not really." He continued, "A couple of years ago a guy walked in and handed me a card with a telephone number on it. He said if anyone came in and asked for Rene, I was supposed to dial his number and leave a message. For this I would be well paid. Thus over the years, I've dialed the number about six times, and usually the next day a man arrives. Rene has been about six different people."

Wally said, "Okay, where can I stay?"

Harry motioned upstairs and said, "We have rooms here."

Wally said, "Great. Now, how about something to eat? I really don't want too much."

Harry said, "How about a nice little fish, some salad, french bread, and maybe our house wine and finish off with coffee?"

Wally said, "Sounds great," and walked over to a table.

Harry walked through the door on the far end of the bar. After eating, Wally went out on the veranda and sat on one of the rocking chairs. He took out a cigar, lit it, and observed the world around him. The sun was reflecting off the sea, and little patterns of light and darkness danced across the surface of the water. The gulls were busy everywhere. Some were perched on the top of the masts of the sailing ships. One or two, patiently waiting for a tasty morsel to be dropped, were circling the fishing boat that was being unloaded.

Chapter 22

Harry White was born and raised on the Atlantic coast not far from Bangor, Maine. His father was a fisherman much like those working on the wharf. However, waters of the Atlantic were not as gentle as here in Narvonne. The winters were bitterly cold. As a young man, he spent much of the time on his father's boat in all types of weather as they worked to obtain a decent catch to make their efforts worthwhile. His father knew the ocean and most of the time brought home a full load in the hold of the fishing boat. On their return to the docks, they would tie up and sell their catch on the spot to the wholesalers, who would either send the fresh fish to market or to a nearby processing plant.

When he was 18, Harry volunteered for the Army. He did well on the battery of tests that he took at the reception center and was assigned to an Officer's Training School. He graduated a Second Lieutenant, was shipped over to Germany and assigned to a commissary outfit. He enjoyed his work because he believed feeding the soldiers was important.

It was by chance that he found the existence of Narvonne. Each time he obtained a leave he came there and stayed at the inn. The inn was in a rundown condition and was operated by an older gentleman. The clientele was local people. Harry got to know the men on the fishing boats and was often invited to go out to sea. He entered into the fishing expeditions with great enthusiasm and earned the respect of the local fishermen.

One day Harry built a contraption out of two steel drums. In the bottom he built a fire, essentially of green wood that he chose very carefully, so that there was more smoke than flame. In the center, he placed on a rack most of the fish that he had thoroughly cleaned. Usually about dusk the men from the boat would join him and sit around the campfire. They would dine on the warm, smoked fish, wine and bread. The fellowship and camaraderie that they had established made Harry feel good. When he first came to this place, he met strangers and now he had friends.

Harry's only extravagances were his trips from Germany to the fishing village. He made it his business to get to know the pilots who were stationed on the base. He did extra favors for people in the right places and so it was not uncommon that he was able to obtain a flight on one of the supply planes to Paris and, on occasion, he might bum a ride on a small aircraft all the way to Marseilles. Harry had saved most of the money the Army had paid him. Upon discharge, instead of going back to the rocky coast of Maine, he headed south to the fishing village. He was able to purchase the Inn at a reasonable price, as the older couple wanted to retire. The first thing he did was refurbish the building inside and out. Although Harry liked to cook and experiment with new types of dishes, he hired a chef.

Harry knew that on each Army base there was an office concerned with recreation for the military on the base. To these offices he sent brochures offering special vacation packages to military personnel and their spouses. Many people took advantage of this offer. It did not make any difference to Harry if his guests were a general and his wife or a private and his wife. Everyone was treated well. Their accommodations were spotless and comfortable. He fed them well. Through hearsay, his business grew and although Harry made money, he treated the local people the same manner he treated more important people.

Harry expanded his business and bought the quaint, rustic building next door. The interior was decorated in the manner of an old country general store that Harry remembered from Maine. He stocked the store with everything he could think of that a tourist might need, from a toothbrush to beach wear.

His pride and joy was an old-fashioned showcase. He stocked this with little candies, which gave great pleasure to the children of the community. They could come in and for the equivalent of about a penny, choose five or six pieces of candy. He took, on consignment, various types of craft projects made by local peasants: seashell sculptures, or relief paintings made from the dried bones of fish. Harry's prices were reasonable, and the business flourished.

When Harry walked out on the veranda and sat next to Wally he said, "I never get tired of this view."

Wally said, "Yes, it is beautiful, isn't it? Is the weather always like this?"

Harry answered, "Yes, most of the time. We do get a few storms once in awhile. Would you like to take a boat ride?"

Wally said, "I do not know anything about boats and I have never been on a small boat. But, why not?"

They got up, walked across the street and down to the end of the wharf. There, tied to the dock, was a brightly painted boat of red, green and white with a tall mast. Harry said to the two young men working on the deck, "Let's take her out."

Harry and Wally boarded the colorful boat. Wally followed Harry forward to what looked like a pilothouse. The two young men untied the bow and stern lines and with a grappling hook, pushed off from the dock. Harry turned the key and started the engine and very soon they were chugging out of the bay. Wally said, "Gee, I thought this was a sailing boat."

Harry answered, "Yes, it is. We use the motor when we are close to shore. Putting the boat exactly where we want is easier, and we do not have to depend on the wind. As soon as we get out a little further, the two sailors you saw will set the sails and we will use the wheel aft to put the boat in the direction we want. In that way, we can watch the sails and see how the wind catches them."

They chugged out a bit further and Harry shut off the motor. He started to walk to the back of the boat, followed by Wally. The two young men had the sails up—a big sail that swung right or left and a smaller sail up in front that was catching the wind and billowing out. When they got to the back and were seated behind the wheel, Harry said, "Now, the front one is the jib—it will billow out and catch the wind. Also, our mainsail will catch the wind, but we use that to tack back and forth. Usually we're able to go on a fairly straight course." When the sails were fully up and they were underway, Harry said, "Come on, move over here. Get behind the wheel."

Wally said, "I don't know how to steer a boat."

Harry said, "Just watch the sails. Get the feel of it," and Wally did.

From time to time Harry would instruct Wally, and they started down the coast, perhaps a half-mile from shore. They could plainly see the buildings, the terrain and the beauty of the shoreline. All of a sudden, Wally turned to Harry and said, "Now look, the wind's blowing in another direction. What do we do, use the motor to come back?"

Harry said, "No, we'll come back the same way, but we'll use a little different tactic."

As they went along, Harry pointed out various communities and after awhile, he pointed toward shore. "There's Port Vendres. In about half a mile, we'll be in Spanish coastal waters."

Wally said, "Do the Spaniards get angry if you sail in their waters?"

Harry said, "There's no problem with fishing boats. It's only the military ships that have to stay out beyond their limit." Harry instructed Wally to slowly do a 90-degree turn and as they did, the sail above their heads moved from one side of the boat to the other. They caught some wind and were off in approximately the same direction from which they came.

Wally said, "You know, I've never done this before, and it's very enjoyable."

Harry said, "Heck, I started steering when I was a kid on my father's fishing boat."

Wally said, "Your Dad was a fisherman?"

Harry said, "Yup, all his life until the time he died, but he fished off the banks of Maine. The weather was a lot harder there than it is here."

They sailed along for a considerable time in silence. Finally Harry said, "What business are you in, if I might ask?"

Wally said, "I work for a real estate company in upstate New York."

Harry said, "Oh. How's business?"

Wally said, "Very good. The economy's been slow but we've been doing all right. We handle a bunch of different kinds of real estate from houses to industrial plants. So we have a variety of customers, and things move along."

Harry said, "I understand from the news that there are a lot of people who are unemployed, crime is high, and it's sort of dog-eat-dog."

Wally said, "Yes, in a way it is. The pace is much faster than here. Also, probably the competition is greater."

Harry thought a minute and said, "We do have competition here, but these fisherman have been working together for so long that if one of them comes in with little or no fish the others share. They've always done that. I don't know if you noticed when you drove up, but we do have some light industry in the community that's only been here a relatively short time. Most of it is the manufacture of small electronic components and things of that nature. I don't think any one company hires over 20 people, but it gives a good base to the area. They're not really competitive because they're building different things."

Harry looked at Wally and said, "What do you say we go in. It's almost dinnertime. We'll feed you a good meal and then, you won't want to miss the sunset. I always like to sit on the veranda and watch. The beautiful rays of color that spread out not only through the sky but also along the water almost look like dancing flames."

After dinner, Wally went out on the veranda to enjoy his cigar with the cup of coffee that he had brought with him. He didn't have to wait too long before the sun started to go down; streaks of yellow and orange, tipped with red, spread across the sky and the reflection on the water was magnificent. He had never seen anything in his life as colorful or as beautiful. The air was clearer, and he felt as if he could see out forever, as there was no blending of earth and sky—just one mass of magnificent color.

After his early drive to the village this morning, the sea breezes, the boat ride and the splendid meal that he had had, Wally felt tired and decided to go up to his bed. His bag had been taken up. His room was bright and airy with a four-poster bed, a sitting area and a desk. He didn't think there was anything in the States that could compare. It didn't take him long to fall fast asleep.

The next morning he arose about seven, showered, shaved, put on a different outfit and went downstairs and sat on the rocker on the veranda. There a young woman, who told him what was on the menu for that morning, served him coffee. He ordered what he thought was a pretty typical American breakfast. Not too long after, she summoned him to the dining room. He sat down and was served and was not disappointed.

Harry came through the door from the kitchen, walked over to Wally and said, "Your man, if he comes, usually arrives about 11."

Wally said, "Great. I think I'll walk over to the fishing boats and watch them get ready to go out."

Harry said, "Most of them have gone, but one or two are a little late this morning, and you'll enjoy seeing them get ready."

Wally approached the first boat. He saw three men busily at work trying to replace a frayed line that ran from the rail up to the top of the mast and back. One man, down on the deck, had just finished making an eye splice in the end of a rope. He put the eye around the wooden peg that was firmly secured into the rail. Wally became interested in watching the man standing at the base of the mast. He had wrapped a rope around the mast several times and then tied it securely around his hips. He did the same with another rope and tied it under his arms. He braced his rubber-soled sneakers against the base of the mast, lifted up the bottom coil around the mast and put pressure on it. He then did the same to the top coil around the mast, repeating the process until he was actually climbing the mast. The man on the deck had secured the other end of the rope onto the peg of the rail. After a few minutes, the man climbing the mast was at the top. He put the end of the long rope through the eye of a bolt that went right through the mast, tied it off, stretching the line as tight as he could. Then he yelled to the people below and dropped the line to the deck. The man who had made the eye splice got the end, put it through a steel loop secured onto the rail, and pulled as tight as he could and tied the rope off.

Wally imagined that this line was to keep the mast steady and help support it, but how much better a steel cable and two turnbuckles would work. He guessed that this was something that had been done for hundreds of years and might never be changed.

A third man was splicing two ends of a rope together. His fingers worked quickly and nimbly and when he was finished, the part that was spliced was not very much bigger than the rope itself. The man started pulling on one part of the rope, and slowly two pulleys rose off the deck. The spliced area passed through the eye of the pulley very easily. Wally guessed that this apparatus was used for raising the nets after they had been cast overboard to bring in the fish. He looked at the men, smiled, raised his thumb up and said the only French word he knew, "Bon."

The men smiled back and shook their heads. Wally then decided to take a look at the store. It was indeed a country store. He had seen many like this on his visits to Vermont. He looked around and saw a display of earrings. One pair caught his eye. They were made out of what appeared to be the shiny, translucent interior of an oyster shell. However, they were a blend of blue, the favorite color of his girlfriend, so he decided to buy them. When he walked over to pay for his purchase, he noticed the old-time, rounded glass showcase. Inside, in neat little crystal dishes were various candies. He decided he would buy some because he hadn't seen anything like that since he was a little boy. He would point at one dish and the woman behind the counter would reach in with what looked like two spoons hinged in the middle, grasp a piece of candy and put it in a bag. Then he would point to another dish. He did this six or seven times. He paid for his purchases and started to walk out of the store. He opened his bag of candy, reached in, pulled one out and put it in his mouth. It had the taste of licorice, but no, he thought, more of an anisette flavor. He walked over to the veranda, enjoying his candy and sat and rocked as he watched the last fishing boat leave the dock. He looked at his wristwatch. It was ten after eleven.

Shortly thereafter, a shiny black car pulled up and parked in front of the Inn. A chauffeur got out and opened the back door. Out stepped a well-dressed middle-aged man who walked up onto the porch watching Wally with every step. When he got near Wally, he said, "My name is Rene, do you wish to speak to me?"

Wally said, "Yes."

The man said, in perfect English, "All right. Let's take a walk."

They walked across the street to the now-deserted wharf. Rene said, "What can I do for you?"

Wally said, "I understand you know how to contact a man named George, alias the Cobra."

The man said, "Maybe I do, maybe I don't. What do you wish?"

Wally hesitated a moment and said, "We have a contract we'd like George to take."

Rene asked, "Who are you? Where are you from, and whom do you represent?"

Wally said, "My name is Walter Monroe, but people call me Wally. I have been sent here by the head of a family in upstate New York. He is the one who wishes George to take the contract."

Rene inquired more about Wally's friends and where he stood in the organization, to make sure that Wally was not an imposter. When they reached the end of the wharf, they sat on benches that were placed there for the convenience of the townspeople to watch the comings and goings of the fishing boats. They faced each other and Rene asked, "Who is the target?"

Wally very quietly and hesitantly said, "The Pope."
Rene looked at him with great surprise and said, "You must be crazy."
Wally said, "No, I'm not. That's the target. My boss seems to think he has good reason to have this done."
Rene said, "If there is such a person as George, or Cobra as you call him, and if he were to take such a contract, it would be very, very expensive."
Wally said, "What's the price?"
Rene looked at him and said, "What are you offering?"
Wally said, "A hundred thousand."
Rene said, after a slight chuckle, "No, my friend, nothing less than $250,000—maybe more."
"Will you contact George," asked Wally, "and get a definite price established?"
Rene nodded his head and added, "I want you to understand something, my friend. If a contract is accepted, I will give you a number. Half of the money will be deposited in that Swiss bank immediately. When the job is done, the other half will be deposited. Failure to do so will lead to more bodies than originally contracted for."
Wally said, "Don't worry. I understand completely." Wally looked at his watch and said, "Look, I can't call my boss for another hour. Why don't we have lunch here at the Inn? How are you going to contact George?"
Rene said, "Don't worry about that. I have a phone in the car."
They walked over to the Inn and had lunch. Nothing was said about the impending agreement during their meal. It was mostly small chitchat. Wally had noticed that the chauffeur had come in on his own and was eating at another table.
The chauffeur had the darkest eyes that Wally had ever seen. When they were finished, Wally again looked at his watch and said; "I think I'll go have a quick smoke on the veranda. Why don't you contact George."
Rene said, "All right. I will."

The chauffeur preceded him out the front door, down the steps and back to the car and sat behind the wheel. Rene got into the passenger side, sat on the front seat, and closed the door. He reached down on the console between the seats and picked up a telephone and pretended to dial, but in reality he was talking to the chauffeur. The chauffeur said, "What did he want?"

Rene looked at the man and said, "George, you'll never believe it. He wants you to take a contract on the Pope."

George continued to stare ahead at the windshield and said, "Very interesting. You know I might just take this contract. I originally set up an assassination on the last Pope, but the guys that were supposed to do it screwed up the deal royally."

George sat there, drumming his fingers on the steering wheel of the car, staring out at the sea. He looked at Rene and said, "I think I'll take the contract."

Rene said, "George, I think you're crazy. I don't think you can trust that egocentric American hood. What if he lets the word out when he's bragging to his friends? They'll have more security around the Pope than you can imagine. It will take an Army to get to him."

George said, "I found out a long time ago a man that can find the right time and the right place can achieve more than two armies." George then asked, "Did he make an offer?"

Rene said, "He started out at $100,000 and I told him it would be over $250,000."

George said, "What do you think?"

Rene said, "It appears to me that this American who wants the job done is really quite emotional about this and would probably go to any expense."

George asked, "Well, what shall we tell him the price is?"

Rene thought for a moment and said, "Would you agree to $400,000?"

George answered, "Considering the risk, yes I think that will be a good fee."

"All right," said George, "why don't you go and tell him."

Rene got out of the car, walked up on the veranda and sat down next to Wally. He leaned over and said, "I talked to my boss on the phone. He will take the contract for $400,000."

Wally's face remained calm and did not show any sign of surprise. Rene glanced toward the car. The sun caused a glare on the windshield and he could not even see George behind the wheel. He was sure that Wally was unaware of what had transpired while he and George were talking.

Wally got up and walked into the Inn, walked over to the bar and said to Harry, "I would like to make a call to the States. How do I dial?"

Harry explained the procedure and gave him the dialing code. As he waited for the call to go through, Wally thought, "Hell, $400,000 . . . . it's no skin off my nose. I did what I was told to do. I made the contact, and I have an answer. I'm in the clear."

Chapter 23

Not long after, the phone rang in Manny's home. Wally was glad that he was up. At least he would not have to put up with another tirade. "Manny, it is Wally."

"How did you do, Wally?"

"Well, I met the contact. We talked for a few minutes; he called his boss, and the answer is 'contract would be accepted and guaranteed for 400 big ones'."

Manny said, "Holy hell, who does he think he is?"

Wally said, "According to the contact that we had through the family, he is the best."

There was silence on the other end of the line while Manny tried to figure out where he would get that kind of money. He had a considerable amount in the safe and more in safe deposit boxes around the city. Yeah, he could do it, so—"All right, Wally. It is a go."

Wally said, "You're sure, boss?"

Manny answered, "Yes, it is a go."

Wally said, "Boss, there is one stipulation. Half of it has to be in a Swiss bank by tomorrow."

Manny thought and said, "Okay."

Wally gave him the name of the bank and the account name and number and then Wally said, "Well, no sense hanging around here. I will try to be home day after tomorrow."

He returned to the veranda and sat down in the rocker, looked at Rene and said, "Okay, you have got the green light. The money will be in the account day after tomorrow and you can check it out."

Rene got up and walked into the Inn. He spread out on the bar five one hundred dollar bills and said to Harry, "This is for services rendered."

Harry did not say a word, scooped up the money, and put it into the cash register. Wally went upstairs, packed his bag, came back downstairs, set the bag down next to the door, and walked over to Harry. He said, "Harry, what do I owe you?"

Harry got out a piece of paper and a pencil, figured it out and showed it to Wally. Wally put the money on the bar plus an extra hundred and said, "This is for the phone call."

Harry said, "Thanks a lot. Nice meeting you."

Wally said, "I have enjoyed meeting you also. Thank you for your kindnesses and especially for that boat trip. I learned a lot. You know, if I were not so tied up where I am, I would come here to live."

Harry said, "We would be glad to have you!"

With that, Wally walked to the door, picked up his bag and walked out to the car. He put the bag on the back seat, got behind the wheel and headed east to Marseilles. Two days later he was back in his hometown, and when he saw Manny, he told him what Rene had said about reneging on the payment. He also repeated that neither of them was to try to contact Rene or George.

Chapter 24

Dick was walking down the main corridor when he saw the man in the black suit and white collar walking in his direction. He thought, "Good Lord, it's Father Jason."

Dick walked toward him. When they were about 10 feet apart, Dick said,

"Father Jason?"

The man looked at him and Dick continued, "What are you doing here?"

Father Jason said, "I could ask you the same question."

Dick said, "Well, I am on my way to Berlin to get some information, if possible, on the subject about which I called you."

Father Jason said, "I am on my way to Palermo on the same mission."

Dick said, "When do you leave for Palermo?"

Father Jason said, "Not until tomorrow morning."

Dick then told him the name of the hotel at which he was staying and said, "I also have a room for Father Stephan. However, he is traveling in civilian clothes, and I thought it would be much better if we did not advertise the fact that he is a member of the clergy."

Dick continued, "I have a two-bedroom suite with more than enough room," and he gave Father Jason his room number. He continued, "Why don't you check into the hotel and tell them you are staying with me. We can use the hotel sort of as the base of our operations. I can leave a message for you or you can leave a message for me. That way we can keep in touch."

Father Jason said, "That sounds like a good idea."

They shook hands and each went off in different directions, each on his own quest.

Father Jason had no trouble checking into Dick's suite. After he showered, he decided he would walk to the Vatican. He wanted to re-familiarize himself with the layout. Jason walked around the large plaza where crowds gathered to be addressed by the Pope or to receive his blessing. Flocks of pigeons soared through the air, landed, and were pecking at the cobblestones trying to find a tasty morsel that someone might have dropped.

After about two hours of walking inside and outside the buildings, he returned to the hotel and placed a call to the monastery in upstate New York. When one of the brothers answered, Father Jason gave him instructions: the brother and five others were to come to Rome. He also told him what equipment to bring. He also suggested that not all of them stay in the same hotel. He gave them the name of the hotel in which he was staying and told them to use the usual procedure on leaving messages.

The next morning Father Jason arose early, packed his few belongings and checked out of the hotel. He stopped in a restaurant and had breakfast, then got a cab and headed for the airport. He found the plane that was going to take him to Palermo was a twin engine, propeller-driven, 12-passenger plane. His seat was right over the wing on the left side. As they soared through the sky, he watched the propeller. If the trip were long, the steady whine of the engine would have put him to sleep. Various thoughts went through his head—not only what he was about, but as he looked at the propeller, he thought, "If that ever came off, would it cut through the plane like a knife or would it go in the opposite direction?"

The plane landed outside Palermo. He hired a car and headed toward the western end of the island and then south to Marsala. On the outskirts of the town, he found what he was looking for, a small Catholic Church, Our Lady of Peace. He decided that the building next to the church was the rectory. They constructed the smaller building of the same material and followed the design of the church.

Father Jason walked up to the front door of the rectory and pulled a cord that he presumed was the bell. Shortly after, the door opened and there stood a man wearing a black cassock. Father Jason knew immediately that this was the person he sought. Jason smiled and said, "Father Giuseppe?"

The man said, "Yes," and looked at Jason quizzically. For a moment there was silence and then Father Jason said, "Joe, how are you?"

Giuseppe knew immediately to whom he was speaking, because Jason was the only one who called him 'Joe.' They had been roommates while studying at the Vatican. Father Joe took a step forward, put his arms around Jason and gave him a bear hug and said, "Jason, it has been a long time." Jason agreed.

Father Joe said, "Come in." They stepped into a large room that was neat and clean, and Jason thought he had stepped back at least 50 years in time. Nothing was as modern as he knew it in the United States.

Father Joe said, "Come, let's go into the kitchen. I was just about to have lunch."

Here again in the kitchen the furniture and appliances were much like those Jason had known growing up. Father Joe went to the cupboard and got another plate and silverware and placed them on the table across from his place setting. Father Joe said, "Jason, sit. Let's eat."

On the table was a block of cheese, sausages, and an array of fruit. In the center was a large, golden-brown loaf of bread that appeared to have been freshly baked. Father Joe took a sharp knife and cut a couple of large slices. In an old country manner, Father Joe speared one of the slices of bread and placed it on Father Jason's plate. He looked at Jason and said, "Will you do the honors?"

Both priests blessed themselves and Jason said, "Bless us, O Lord, for these Thy gifts which we are about to receive from Thy infinite bounty, through Christ our Lord, Amen."

While they ate, they reminisced about their school days and some tricks they had played on other students. As the conversation progressed, the subject changed as to what was currently happening in their lives. Each man was very interested in the other as they had been friends for a long time. This was an opportunity to catch up on the other's career and interests. When they were finished, Father Jason said, "This has been an excellent meal. It is a wonder you are not fat, eating like this."

Father Joe said, "Our food is simple, but usually tasty and enjoyable. Would you believe that all of this," making a gesture with his hands over the food, "comes from right around here and not out of cans?"

Father Jason said, "I am afraid we would be lost if we did not have canned food in the United States. It is much better to get everything fresh."

When they were finished, Father Jason and Father Joe took what was left in their wine glasses and went into the parlor. When they were comfortably seated, Father Joe asked, "What can I do for you? I know that this is not a social visit. You were never one to spend your time on that."

Father Jason said, "I am here to try to meet a man named Dominick Giovanni."

Father Joe was quite surprised and he said, "Do you know who this man is?"

Jason said, "I think I have an idea."

Father Joe continued, "He is the Don of Dons, the supreme power. He is the one who judges when there is a conflict between families. He has the power to reach out to almost anywhere in the world and his word is usually law. Of course, there are many who would like to usurp his power, so he is always well guarded."

"Do you know him," asked Jason, "personally, I mean?"

Father Joe said, "Yes, on occasion he comes to my church, so I have gotten to know him, and he has been quite generous."

Jason asked, "Could you make arrangements for me to see him?"

Joe said, "We will see if he will receive you."

Father Joe walked over to an old-fashioned roll top desk. He opened it, sat on a chair in front of the desk, got a sheet of paper and a pen and wrote a note. He put the note in an envelope and sealed it. On the front he put the Don's name. He got up and started to walk toward the door and said to Father Jason, "Come on, and let's take a walk."

Chapter 25

Father Joseph took his biretta off a peg next to the doorjamb and put it on his head. He told Jason that he would not need his car, that his destination was within walking distance.

After they had walked about one quarter of a mile, they came to a gas station and garage. Jason thought the place had seen better days. The single pump, once painted white and green, was now speckled with rust. Through the large open door, he could see a man working on a motor scooter. Father Joe approached the man and, in his native language, asked if someone could do an errand for him. The man called out and soon his son responded. He walked up to Father Joseph and greeted him. The priest extended the letter and asked him if he would please deliver it to the home of Dominick Giovanni. He instructed the young man to wait for an answer. The boy said he would, rolled a motor scooter out of the side of the garage, hopped on it and sped away up the hill.

Returning to Father Joseph's home, Joe said, "Let us gather some payment for the young man."

Father Jason said, "What do you mean, 'gather payment'? Do you have money growing on trees?"

Father Joe said, "No. You will see."

Instead of going through the front door of the house, they walked around to the back porch. Father Jason was quite surprised when he saw a garden arranged in neat rows. Although small, the garden seemed to be very productive. Father Joe walked up onto the porch and took down a large cloth bag. He said, "Come, let us pick some vegetables."

They picked several varieties of what Father Jason believed was squash. In addition, there were cucumber-like vegetables, and these were added to the bag. Jason held the bag open as Father Joe gathered up a large bunch of greens. The bag was nearly filled, and then he picked several large, bright red, plump tomatoes.

"There," Father Joseph said, "that should be sufficient. Why don't you hold these while I gather some flowers?"

Jason said, "Flowers, too?"

Father Joe said, "Jason, you cannot live by bread alone."

They walked to the back door of the house and into the kitchen. Father Joseph took a knife and cut the ends of the flowers. He then went over behind the cupboard and got a newspaper that he dampened. He rolled up the flowers in the paper so they would stay fresh. These he put on top of the bag. When he was finished, he turned to Jason and said, "How would you like some iced tea?"

Jason was a bit warm from the walk to the garage and the chore in the garden and said, "That would be great."

Father Joseph went to the refrigerator and got out a pitcher of iced tea. He filled two glasses. He handed one to Jason, and the other he put on the table in front of him.

Jason said, after his first taste, "This is delicious. There is just enough lemon to quench the thirst."

While they drank their tea, they talked about the problems facing the church and changes that could occur. They discussed the conservative church leaders and then those who were liberal. They found they agreed about the way various people were trying to cause change. About 40 minutes later, the young man from the garage knocked on the door. Father Joe told him to come in, and he handed the priest a note. Father Joseph got up and got the bag with the vegetables and the flowers. The young man started to protest but Father Joseph persisted in the other direction. Finally the young man acknowledged he had lost the argument, took the bag and told Father Joseph that he would return the bag promptly. Father Joseph poured two more glasses of tea and sat.

He slowly opened the letter. On the envelope was his name: "Father Giuseppe Ventre." Joseph read the note to Jason. It said that Don Giovanni would be happy to greet the priest the next morning.

Father Joseph looked up at Jason and said, "Well, I think that is all set, and of course, you will spend the night here in my spare bedroom. We will have dinner, if you can put up with my cooking, and maybe we can take a short walk and go over to the church, which I really want you to see."

Father Jason was astonished that the front door of the church was unlocked. As they entered the building, he felt its cool, still peaceful atmosphere. Up over the old-fashioned altar was a carved crucifix. Father Joseph explained to him that it had been made out of one piece of wood. The altar itself was constructed of wood, and on the front were carvings of scenes from the Bible. Along the walls were paintings depicting the Stations of the Cross. These, also, were framed in highly polished wood and were artistically constructed. He saw beauty everywhere he looked. When he mentioned this to Father Joseph, Joseph said, "The people who originally created this gave the best of their talents for the honor and glory of God."

Father Joe stood and watched as Jason inspected every detail with care. Finally Father Jason turned to the parish priest and said, "You know, I cannot believe this. I do not think I have ever seen a more beautiful church."

Father Joseph said, "Thank you, but come, let's go to the choir loft."

They walked to the back of the church and up a set of stairs to the loft. There, standing off to one side, was an old-fashioned pump organ. Father Jason said, "How old is that?"

Joseph said, "I really do not know. Maybe a hundred years or so."

Father Joseph walked over and sat on a stool in front of the pump organ. He looked up at Jason and said, "What would you like? Bach? A hymn? Or jazz?"

Father Jason said, "You must be kidding . . . . jazz?"

Father Joseph said, "Look, Jason, we might be here in rural Europe, but we do get news of the outside world once in awhile, and you know that I have always liked music."

Father Joseph started to pump the pedals and when he played a jazz rendition of *I Ain't Got Nobody*. Both smiled and broke into laughter. When Father Joseph was finished, Father Jason said, "Hey, that was great, just great. As they say back in the states, you really know how to tickle those ivories!"

Father Joseph looked down and said, "I guess they are real ivories. They must have been because they did not have plastic back then."

Both went down the stairs and back to the rectory but before they did, they walked up to the altar rail, knelt, blessed themselves and prayed silently. Joseph prayed for his flock; Father Jason that his task would end peacefully and successfully.

At the rectory, Jason said, "I will help you cook dinner," and he did.

Dinner was late, and afterwards they sat in the living room and talked, each enjoying a glass of the local wine. Both had had a busy day and they turned in early.

The next morning they had a breakfast of fresh rolls and homemade jam, served to Father Joseph by one of his parishioners. At the door, Jason shook hands with Father Joseph and said, "I do not know when I will be back but I will be sure to stop, even for a moment, before I leave the island."

Jason went out, got into his car, and followed the instructions given him by Father Joseph on how to find Don Giovanni's home. As he drove, Father Jason thought about the day before. He did not think he had ever had a more diverse or pleasant day than being with Father Ventre, from picking vegetables in a garden, to enjoying the beauty of a small church, and rekindling the friendship of so long ago. He thought, "Today, I am a happy man, but now I must face a task that I do not really relish."

As he drove along the highway, the vista opened. He could see that he was not very far from the cliff that went down to the sea on his right side. On his left the large hills sloped up from the highway. He was really enjoying the drive. About 20 minutes later he saw the entrance to Don Giovanni's home, which Father Joe had described to him. There was a large, circular area in front of the gate. Around the property was a stonewall at least 10-12 feet high. On top of the wall were supports that leaned out over the wall and attached to these were four strands of barbed wire. He thought he saw the reflection of the sun off pieces of broken glass on top of the wall. He pulled right up to the gate. Just inside a cubicle stood a man. As Jason drew near, the man asked who Jason was and what he wanted. Jason identified himself and told the man he was expected. The man said, "Just a moment."

Jason got back into his car and settled behind the wheel. He thought, "I wonder what happens next."

Chapter 26

The offices of the Secretary of State were located in the Vatican palace. Cardinals Vellini, Burns and Salvemini were seated around a table. At the end of the table was Dr. Santos. Cardinal Vellini told the other three about Father O'Connor's willingness to act as a kidney donor. Dr. Santos said, "Yes, he came to see me, and I explained to him that he should have no problems living a full and active life with one kidney. He seems to be a dedicated young man."

Cardinal Vellini responded, "Yes he is." Looking down at a legal size pad, he said to the others, "I had a call from the Bishop in New York State. The bishop's secretary was also on the phone. He stated that this man's likeness to the Pope was so close that they had to alter his appearance while he traveled. The secretary thought many people would recognize the double as the Pope, and they did not want this to happen. He will be checking into his hotel tomorrow and will call us after he arrives. The man's name is Father Stephan Zablonski. He has been a priest for a long time and teaches at a university in New York. He is quite fluent in languages and church history. A friend of his arrived day before yesterday and arranged for their stay at the hotel. This man's name is Dick Rogers. My secretary called the hotel to contact Mr. Rogers. He left a message that he would be gone for the day and not be back until late tomorrow afternoon or early evening. I believe the plan is that the following day both will arrive here in this office at my invitation. They will be in civilian clothes and will represent themselves as American businessmen. Mr. Rogers has been a very successful entrepreneur, an expert in computers; and both of you know," looking at the other two Cardinals, "we have been interested in upgrading some of the computers in our offices."

Cardinal Vellini turned his attention to Dr. Santos and said, "Doctor, can you give us a status report?"

Dr. Santos said, "Yes. The Pope has reacted well to new antibiotics and we now have his infection under control. I think, now that we have a donor, and that the stand-in is arriving, we should arrange for the Pope to be taken to the hospital."

Cardinal Burns said, "Yes, indeed. We should do this under the greatest security." He continued, "I have not had the opportunity to tell anyone yet, but I have received word from very good sources that someone plans the Pope great harm. They may even try to assassinate him, so the sooner we get him to a hospital where we know we can have enough security people, the better."

Dr. Santos said, "Yes, we could move him tonight. I have a van at our disposal. However, in reality, it is a well-equipped ambulance. We can drive up to the back of the Vatican palace and use the freight elevator that goes all the way up to his floor."

Cardinal Burns said, "That sounds like a good idea. There is one thing that bothers me. The man who is going to replace the Pope may be in jeopardy, but we can try to give him as much protection as possible."

That evening, Cardinal Vellini, Dr. Santos, and the Pope's aide were in the Pope's bedroom. The Pope was in bed. Dr. Santos and the aide lifted the Pope up on a gurney, and he started to cover himself with the blankets. The Pope said to Cardinal Vellini, "You may need this," and extended his hand. Cardinal Vellini reached out and the Pope dropped his Papal ring into the outstretched palm of the Cardinal. They finished covering the Pope with blankets, snugged up the straps to hold him securely, and wheeled him to the elevator and down to the street level. The gurney was gently placed through the back doors of the van and secured to the floor. Dr. Santos got in with the aide, as they had instructed the driver not to get out of the van. The doors were closed and the van drove off to the hospital.

Chapter 27

Although the security at the Berlin airport was much stricter than at many other airports, Dick was able to get through very rapidly. He hailed a cab and gave the cabby an address in the eastern section of the city. When they arrived, he asked the cabby to stop. He looked out at a large, two-story house with a mansard roof. He asked the cabby to wait, got out of the car, surveyed the house, and walked around to the back. Sure enough, the lean-to porch was still there and he looked up at the window above the porch and smiled.

* * *

Dick and Nickolai were tracking down the group of black marketeers and a man by the name of Frankel, the brain behind the outfit. They put him under constant surveillance. They followed him to this house that he had frequented on a regular basis. Dick and Nickolai thought it might be the center of their operation. They sat and waited in their car until almost 1:00 a.m. and then decided to find out what went on inside the house. They knew they could not get into the front or side of the building without being discovered, so they walked around the back. On the side of the back porch was a drainpipe going up to the very steep roof. It was securely fastened so both were able to climb up the pipe to the roof. The window had not been locked, so very quietly, they opened it and went in. Both drew their guns. They found themselves at the end of a long hallway with many doors on both the left and right sides. Whispering very quietly, they decided to check out each individual room. They came to the first door and opened it cautiously. Inside, the room was pitch black, so Dick felt on the wall for the light switch. When the light went on, a woman jumped out of bed, throwing the covers back. She was completely nude and she ran for the door, screaming at the top of her voice. The man in the bed wore only a pair of shorts and his socks and he went running out, yelling for help. Very soon, all the doors opened and men and women in various modes of dress and undress came yelling into the hall. At the far end of the corridor a male voice started shouting, "Stand where you are or I will shoot!"

Dick and Nickolai both realized that with the panic going on in the hall, this man would not dare fire. They ran to the window, got onto the low, slanted roof and jumped the six feet to the ground. When they hit, they rolled to break their fall, got up, ran to their car and drove away.

* * *

As Dick continued to look at the back of the house, he chuckled and remembered how he and Nickolai, when they finally got to their car, laughed hysterically. What they hoped was a den of thieves, had turned out to be a bordello. As they drove, Dick had said, "We should not tell anyone about this experience, or we will never live it down," and they continued to laugh.

Dick walked back to his cab, got in, looked at his watch and knew he still had time. He had decided not to call Nickolai, but to try to surprise him at a restaurant where he usually had lunch. He said to the driver,

"Go to checkpoint Charlie."

The driver turned and said, "It is no longer there."

Dick said, "I know, but go to where it was."

When they arrived at the place that used to be the passage into the East, the cabby stopped. Dick again asked him to wait, and got out of the car. He walked across the bridge to where the large wall had stood. He could still see traces of the foundation in the ground. Like a young boy, he put one foot on one side of the foundation, spread his legs wide, and put the other foot on the other side. He thought, "Ironically I can do this today, but when I was here 20 years ago machine guns would be ripping up the earth around me."

He stood there like that for a moment, then decided to go and find Nickolai. The cab stopped in front of the little restaurant where Nickolai and Dick had their first meeting. He got out of the cab, paid his fare and the cab drove off. Dick turned toward the restaurant and above the door was the sign, "Haufbrau." He entered the door as a little bell chimed to announce his arrival. He looked around the room. It was a typical little German restaurant. Although the place was busy, Dick spotted Nickolai over in a corner. He slowly walked to Nickolai's table and when he got about two paces away he said, "Nicky, how are you doing?"

Nickolai looked up, and a broad smile came across his face. He rose, gave Dick a big bear hug, and they sat down at the table. A waitress appeared and Dick ordered lunch. Nickolai also asked for a small glass, which the server brought. On the table was a silver pocket flask that Dick recognized immediately. Nickolai always liked to have a little vodka with his meal and this restaurant did not sell liquor. When the waitress brought the glass, Nickolai poured about a half teaspoon of vodka into the bottom of the glass. He set the flask down and they raised their glasses to one another, clinked them, and drank the contents. Nickolai knew that Dick was a diabetic; however, this ritual had started years ago. It was their way of saluting one another. Dick said to Nickolai, "Are you still in the spy business?"

Nickolai responded, "No, no longer. There is really no need, and what they still do; I leave to the younger boys. I am now in charge of stimulating foreign investments in Russia. I'm permanently stationed here in Berlin. I meet with businesspeople from all over the world and try to get them to either invest in my country or buy the materials."

Dick said, "Are you still a colonel?"

Nickolai said, "No, I am now a two star general. I do not have any authority, but it really helps in Russia. I have a bigger problem with the bureaucrats in Moscow than I do with the foreign investors. They just do not understand capitalism."

Nickolai then said to Dick, "What are you doing now? Are you still in business?"

Dick explained that when he got out of the Army he started to go into designing and programming computers and that he had now turned his business over to several younger men, but still he got royalties. He also told him about his work with Father Stephan in research. Nickolai said, "Is it interesting?"

Dick replied, "Very. You know it is good to know how various ideas started. They are so different from our earlier beliefs."

Their lunches were served. They ate heartily, chatting and reminiscing about the days when they worked together and how each tried to outdo the other. Dick told him about his stop at checkpoint Charlie and about his visit to the old house and both laughed. When they were finished with their meal and were enjoying their coffee, Nick said, "Well, old friend, what is the real reason that brings you to Berlin?"

Dick became very serious and said, "Nicky, if you wanted to have a well-known and respected individual assassinated, who do you think would take the job?"

Nickolai raised his arm and rubbed his chin with his index finger. He was in deep thought. Finally he said, "There is a man they call George, George the Cobra. Somebody pinned that name on him a long time ago. It was because he struck so fast and could then slither off into the darkness so that nobody knew who he was or what he looked like." He paused a minute, then said, "Except me."

Dick asked, "Was he one of yours?"

Nickolai said, "Yes. For a long time until he became a rogue and took contracts on his own. I lost several good men because of him. I finally decided that someone else would catch up with him eventually."

Dick asked, "What does he look like?"

Nickolai said, "Medium height, medium build. Probably dark hair, slightly graying." Then he added, "The physical description will do you no good. He is a master at disguise and can make himself look heavier. He can change his appearance. The most important things that might help identify him are his dark, piercing eyes; darker than I have ever seen."

Dick said, "Do you know where I can find him?"

Nickolai gave him an address in Marseilles but then he added, "You probably could contact him better in a fishing village near Norborne."

Nicky gave Dick the same instructions he had received. Dick said, "Where did you find this person?"

Nicky said, "Let's go for a walk and enjoy the sunshine, and I will tell you the story."

Dick said, "Why don't you finish your coffee. I am going to try to make a telephone call. Maybe I will get lucky."

Dick went over to the bartender and, after a brief conversation, was shown to a small room that looked like an office. On the desk was a telephone that he used to place a call to his hotel in Rome. He was lucky, for a few minutes later the person at the desk answered. Dick left a message for Father Jason. When the desk clerk read the message back Dick said, "Good. That is the way I want it."

The message had been quite cryptic. Dick returned to the bar and paid their checks. He also gave additional money for the telephone call.

Nicky rose and started to walk toward him. They walked out of the restaurant and onto the street. Not too far down was a grassy area with trees and they sat on a bench. Nicky started to talk about George.

George's father was German and his mother came from a Slavic country. The father worked, he believed, for the railroad, so would be away from home for several days at a time. The mother, an attractive blond, had married George's father thinking she could enjoy what she thought was the good life. Instead, when the father came home from his trips, he would drink heavily. When he got drunk, he would become angry and many times George and his mother felt his father's wrath. George's mother felt she wanted more from life than an abusive husband and the drudgery of taking care of George and the house. When the father left on one of his trips, she decided to go out one evening to one of the local clubs. She enjoyed herself and came home just before dawn. This habit of going out became more and more frequent. George had to rely on his own instincts to take care of himself. There were times when he would not see his mother for two or three days. George got into all sorts of trouble—petty thievery, assault and battery and once he was accused of attempted murder. There was not enough evidence on the last charge, so he was released. George seemed to have no sense of right or wrong and took on almost any task if it paid well enough. Nicky said, "He was about 19 when one of my agents hired him to beat up a man to keep him in line. That's when he came to my attention." Nicky added, "I recruited him and we ran him through the school and you know what happens there. He became quite proficient in all types of tradecrafts. He worked for us for about eight years and then decided to take jobs on his own. And as I said before, we lost several good men trying to bring him back in, and then decided that we would leave him to his own devices. I must warn you, Dick, he is good."

Dick looked at Nicky and said, "I believe our man is better."

Nicky asked, "Are you staying overnight?"

Dick said, "No, my friend." Looking at his watch, he added, "I leave in about two and one half hours. This is important and I have to keep on top of it."

They sat and talked for another half hour, and when Dick noticed a cab pull up and discharge some passengers, he waved. Nicky walked Dick to the cab, and opened the door. Then Nicky gave him a typical bear hug and they shook hands. Nicky said, "Goodbye, my friend. Don't wait so long for your return visit."

Dick answered, "I hope your business brings you to America and you can stay for awhile."

Dick got into the cab and it drove off. Nicky walked slowly back to his office.

Chapter 28

Bob and Beau found the stub of a paycheck in O'Neill's personal effects and decided to visit the employer. When they got to the proper address, Beau parked in front of a store. On a large glass window was painted *Feathers & Fur Pet Shop*. As they walked through the door, a small bell overhead tinkled. To the left of the store, a middle-aged salesperson was showing a small black and white kitten to a much younger woman. The squirming kitten had four white paws and a white face. The younger woman tried several times to scratch the kitten's head but had no success. The salesperson put the little kitten back inside its cage with the mother cat and four little sleeping kittens. When the black & white kitten entered the cage, he made a dash for his mother to get something to eat. The younger woman said, "No wonder he squirmed. He was hungry."

From around the corner toward the back of the store came an older man who was dressed in work clothes. He had clearly been working in the back of the store. As he approached the detectives, he asked, "May I help you?"

Beau and Bob identified themselves and showed their shields. Beau asked, "Did you once have a person by the name of O'Neill working here?"

The man thought for a moment and then said, "Yes. Yes, we did. He did fairly well."

Bob said, "What did he do?"

The man answered, "He kept the place neat, cleaned the cages, fed the animals, and when a truck would come in with supplies, he would unload it and put every item in its proper place."

Beau said, "What kind of worker was he?"

The man answered, "Not bad."

"Do you have any information on him," asked Bob?

The man said, "Wait a minute." He went to a file cabinet and pulled out a folder. On the outside tab was marked "O'Neill." He handed it to the detectives. Beau put it on the counter top and started to leaf through the papers. Inside were W-4 and W-2 forms, medical application, and finally a reference letter from a pet shop in Buffalo, New York.

Beau asked, "Did you check his reference?"

The man answered, "In all honesty, no. He was never near the cash register, and he usually left before we did when we locked the store up for the night. So I did not."

Beau said, "May I have this?"

The man said, "Sure."

Beau asked, "Did you let him go?"

The man said, "No, he just did not come around anymore. In fact, we owe him two days' salary. He was a kind of odd duck. He stayed by himself and never really entered into any conversation. I do not think the man spoke more than three or four sentences to me."

"Okay," Bob said, "I think we have enough. Thank you very much."

As they were walking out, Beau noticed several large tanks of tropical fish. He turned around and said to the man, "You know, you should change your sign."

The man said, "How come?"

Beau said, "Well, with the fish, you ought to name your store *'Feather, Fur and Scales'*."

The man chuckled and said, "I will think about it."

When they were back in their car, Beau looked at Bob and said, "I think we ought to contact the Buffalo P.D."

Bob said, "You are reading my mind."

When the two detectives got back to their office, Beau placed a call to the homicide division of the Buffalo police department.

On the other end of the line was a Lieutenant Pitock. Beau identified himself and said, "I would like to ask you a strange question. Have you got an open case involving the murder of a nun?"

There was silence for several moments on the other end of the line. Finally the Lieutenant answered,

"Not only one, but two."

As he talked, Beau scribbled a note and handed it over to Bob. Bob listened intently as Beau asked questions. Beau asked, "Did the nuns have duct tape over their mouths?"

Beau wrote, "yes," on the pad.

"Were their arms tied behind them with a piece of cord that looked like clothesline?"

Beau wrote, "yes" on the pad.

"Was a knife used?"

Beau wrote, "yes" on the pad.

"Did death occur from the knife wound projected upward under the rib cage?"

Again, Beau wrote "yes."

Beau then said, "I think you can close your file. We had one murder of a nun with the same m.o., and then we had an attempted murder of another nun. However, someone shot the perpetrator. It looks as though we can wind this up also."

Before he hung up, he asked the Lieutenant the dates on which the murders occurred. Putting the phone back in its cradle, he clapped his hands together and said,

"Hot damn."

Dick said, "One more call, huh?"

Beau answered, "Yes," and began dialing. When the other party answered, Beau identified himself and stated they were doing a routine investigation and could they please tell him if they had a man by the name of O'Neill working for them in the past. If so, could they tell him the dates of employment?

Beau listened and wrote little notes on the yellow pad in front of him. He then said, "Thank you," and hung up the phone. He turned to Dick and said, "The dates coincide. Buffalo can put this case to bed and shortly, we can too." He continued, "What do you think we should do?"

Dick thought for a moment and then said, "I think we should chalk this baby up to justifiable homicide and close the case. I do not think we will ever find the guy that knocked off O'Neill. He did society a big favor."

Beau said, "I agree wholeheartedly. Let's go talk to the Lieutenant."

Chapter 29

After the gates were open to Dominick Giovanni's home, Father Jason drove about a quarter of a mile before he reached the house. The grounds were extremely well kept and on the way in he saw two different men walking around the area. One man was carrying a shotgun in the crook of his arm. Another had a gun slung over his shoulder with a piece of rope. Father Jason could see that these were not the typical hunting shotguns, but had very short barrels. The driveway swung around in front of the house and then came back upon itself in a large circle. In the center of that circle was a statue with a bubbling fountain. There was a flagstone patio across the front of the house and along the right side. At its edge were boxes containing beautiful flowers. Father Jason pulled into the parking area next to a Jeep. He got out and started to walk toward the right side of the house. Two steps led to the top of the patio and as he ascended these, a gray haired man approached him. The man was dressed in jeans and a rumpled shirt and he wore a pair of sandals. He was not a very big man, but had the rugged look of someone who had worked in the fields. As he approached Father Jason, he extended his hand, and said, in perfect English, "I am Dominick Giovanni."

Father Jason grasped his hand, shook it firmly and said, "I am Father Jason."

For a man his age, Giovanni had a firm grasp and his skin was hard and callused. Dominick said, "Come and join me for a cup of coffee."

They walked along the patio to an awning-covered area. Around the table were several wicker chairs. Giovanni said, "Sit," and motioned to another man who brought them both coffee. As Father Jason sat there, he looked out over the lawns and gardens. Off to the side of the house was a square pool with a fountain in the center. Around the pool was a flagstone walkway and along the walk were beds of flowers. Out in the distance he could see what he thought were grapevines, hung from wires, strung between posts. He looked at Giovanni and said, "You have a magnificent place."

Giovanni said, "Thank you. I like it here. I looked a long time for this spot. The mountain rises behind the house, and out across the road as the cliff drops down to the sea. It is a secure place."

Father Jason said, "Speaking of security, as I drove in here I noticed that you are well protected."

Giovanni answered, "That is necessary as there are those who would like to see me dead. Nevertheless, tell me, Father, what may I do for you?"

Father Jason answered, "This is a courtesy visit. I come to you out of respect for your position. It seems your nephew, Manny Salvador, has found someone, or is looking for someone in Europe to assassinate the Pope."

Using his formal title, Jason said, "Don Giovanni, if Salvador is successful in having his plans carried out, I wanted to advise you that he will not live to see his next birthday. I do not wish to see a vendetta against the Church or members of the Church."

Don Giovanni shook his head up and down slowly and said, "I have heard about the problem he has had with several of his factories, and there has been a rumor about his fight with the church to get an annulment."

After a long pause, he continued, "Manny has not really been very stable over the years. I told him when he was a young man that his temper would be his undoing."

Giovanni continued, "You know, I have searched out this place and thought I would live my life in quiet and peace. Every day I go down and tend to my grapes. I live quietly, but there are those who want to keep stirring the pot until it boils over. I have long wished that Tony had been the eldest in his family, so that he could have taken over the business. It would have been run more smoothly and without as many problems."

After a few minutes of silence, Father Jason said, "There probably is no way to have a contract canceled if it has been established."

Giovanni answered, "Once a contract is in place it will be carried out, but at this time we have no idea the who, why, where or what."

Father Jason said, "I have a friend who is trying to find out those details right now. If I might use your telephone, I would like to call my hotel in Rome and see if I have any messages."

Don Giovanni motioned to a phone and Father Jason dialed the hotel number. He asked for his messages and then said, "Thank you," and hung up the phone. He said to Don Giovanni, "My friend had good fortune. A person by the name of George is going to handle the contract."

Don Giovanni said, "George, better known as the Cobra, is a very dangerous man."

Father Jason told Don Giovanni the place and the manner in which a person could contact George. Giovanni said, "I suppose you will follow this through and try to make contact?"

Father Jason said, "Yes, I will go back and say goodbye to my friend Father Joseph and then get a plane to Rome."

Don Giovanni said, "I think I have a better idea. You can call your friend and say goodbye from here and we will take care of your transportation directly to the coast of France."

He motioned to the man who had brought the coffee. The man went out and was gone for several moments. When he returned, he placed an article wrapped in cloth in front of Father Jason. Giovanni said, "You are going into a very dangerous area and you might need this."

He suggested that Father Jason should unwrap the cloth, which he did. On the table was an automatic with an extra clip.

Don Giovanni said, "I know from your record that you are capable and familiar with the use of such a firearm."

Father Jason looked puzzled and asked, "What do you mean, 'by my record'?"

Don Giovanni answered, "Well, when I got Father Joseph's note asking me to see you, I made a call. Knowing people in the right places, with enough money and in this age of computers, not much can be kept a secret. I know about your Army service record and your abilities in the field."

He continued, "As you have done your background checks, so I have done my homework. About three miles from here, my boat is tied up to the dock. You will be taken directly to the French coast and dropped off in a quiet area so you do not have to be concerned about passing through customs."

Father Jason called his friend and said his goodbyes. He said he was sorry that he could not come and see him again, but that they had arranged transportation for him and that he hoped it would not be too long before they could get together again. When he was finished with his telephone call, Don Giovanni said, "Do not worry about your car. It will be returned. Whatever happens, do not worry about a vendetta. Good luck to you, my friend. Be careful. Watch your back. You are entering a den of vipers."

Father Jason picked up the clip for the automatic and put it into his pocket. He saw that a holster had been provided. He hooked it onto his belt and slid the gun in place. Don Giovanni motioned to two men who escorted Father Jason to the Jeep. Father Jason sat in the passenger seat as one man drove and the other sat in the back. Down on the floor, Jason noticed another sawed-off shot gun. They drove out of the driveway and onto the highway. Several miles up, they pulled off into a parking area. There was a small building and Jason could see that a set of stairs led down to a beach area. Moored at the end of the dock was a cabin cruiser that looked to be about 25 or 30 feet long. The three of them boarded the boat. A man was standing at the wheel in the cabin and another man was on deck. He was untying the forward line. The man in the cabin switched on the engines while the other man untied the aft line. Slowly the boat moved out to the open water. When the cruiser was several hundred yards offshore, the captain pulled back the throttles and the boat leapt forward. He had to brace himself against the surge of power as they literally flew across the water. Father Jason turned to the man standing next to him and asked, "How many engines does this boat have?"

The man answered, "Two. Two big diesels. We can do about 30 knots." He added, "Padre, if you are hungry, there is coffee and food down below, or if you had like to stretch out and rest, there are also bunks."

Father Jason said, "No, I would rather stay up here on deck and watch the scenery. I really enjoy the water and do not have much opportunity in my life to do this sort of thing. Maybe I will have a cup of coffee later. Thank you very much."

Jason walked to the rear of the boat and sat on one of the well-padded benches. The man Jason had been talking to joined him, sat down, and lit his cigar. Several hours later, the man pointed toward what looked to be the vague outline of the shore and said, "There is the coast of France. It will not be long before we dock."

Jason said, "I think I will go down now and get a cup of coffee. Would you like some?"

The man shook his head no. Jason went below and found a very compact, but an efficient cabin. On each side were double bunks. At the end was a very small kitchenette. A metal frame held the glass coffee pot so it would not slip off the coffee maker. He looked at it for a moment and then figured out how it worked. He opened the frame and poured himself a cup of coffee into a large mug, put back the frame, walked back up to his seat in the rear of the boat, and enjoyed the coastline as it appeared to become closer and closer. About 45 minutes later the captain had throttled back on the engines, and they were headed for a point on shore. The man who had been keeping Father Jason company said,

"Our Captain knows exactly where he is. He has made runs on this coast often. You will be about 30 miles from your destination and we do have a car available for you."

The man continued, "We are going to stop as if to refuel. While they are pumping the fuel into the tank, you can go up on the dock as if you want to stretch your legs. You should walk back and forth. Try to be as inconspicuous as possible. The car you want is the gray one. Here are the keys."

Father Jason took the keys and put them in his pocket. When they pulled up to the dock near the fuel pump, and the deck hand tied up the boat, Father Jason did as he was instructed. He got up on the dock and walked back and forth slowly as if he were observing the sea gulls and the buildings on the shore. Finally he walked very slowly toward the parking area at the end of the dock. The two men at the pump were busy with their chores. When Father Jason reached the parking area he saw the gray sedan and walked toward it. He inserted the key in the lock, opened the door and got in. He sat there for some moments, then started the car and drove off. About 40 minutes later, he pulled up in front of White's Inn.

Chapter 30

On his flight back to Rome, Dick thought about his old friend Nickolai. It had been good to see him after such a long time. He was happy that he was able to persuade Nicky not to interfere in the assassination plot. If anything had gone wrong, Nicky would have suffered and an international scandal could have occurred. No, he thought, it is better that we let Father Jason take care of it. If anything were ever made public, it would be a case of keeping it in the family.

When he got back to his hotel, Dick knocked on Father Stephan's door. It was opened almost immediately and there stood Father Stephan, but he did not look like his old friend. He was still wearing the disguise. Father Stephan asked,

"Where have you been? All you said in your note was 'off to Berlin'."

Dick said, "I went to see an old friend. I was sure he could give me some information and he did."

Dick related all that had happened with Nicky, then asked, "Are you sure Jason got the information?"

Dick answered, "The desk clerk gave me a message. All it said was 'on my way. J.S.', so I assume he did."

Stephan said, "I hope nothing happens to him."

Dick asked, "What is happening with you?"

Father Stephan replied, "I made the telephone call as I was supposed to, and the Vatican is sending a car in the morning. I am supposed to bring all my luggage, but I want you to go with me also. Will you?"

Dick said, "Certainly. Do you know what they have in mind for you, Steph?"

"Not really," said Father Stephan, "but I imagine we will find out soon enough."

The next morning Dick left his room and knocked on Father Stephan's door. Father Stephan opened it, bag in hand. Dick said, "Let's go down and have breakfast and then we can check you out."

Father Stephan said, "That's okay by me."

After breakfast they checked Stephan out, and walked through the front door of the hotel. Standing at the curb was a car from the Vatican. The chauffeur was standing along the side of it, waiting for them. They walked up to him and the man asked, "Mr. Rogers?"

Dick said, "Yes." The chauffeur opened the back door and gestured for them to get in. Then he put the bag in the trunk of the car. After that, he got in and drove the car toward Vatican City. Soon they were driving in front of St. Peter's Basilica. The driver cut in on a small roadway. Behind the Basilica were formal gardens and quiet streets with buildings of all types of architectural design. They drove up to a parking space near a very large building. Dick said, "I guess this is it, the Vatican Palace."

It was several buildings joined together, surrounding a courtyard. The building had more than 1,000 rooms. In one section of the palace was the Pope's apartment. Not far away were the apartment and offices of the Secretary of State, Cardinal Vellini. In addition, there were more apartments, offices and chapels. The palace housed one of the most complete libraries in the world and was open to scholars from all nations to do research. In another section were housed a museum and the archives of the Church with documents and books going back hundreds of years. The interior walls were adorned with priceless works of art. In various alcoves and in corners were beautiful pieces of sculpture. Dick thought, "This indeed, is a palace."

The chauffeur walked up to a man in uniform and handed

him the bag. Then he turned toward Dick and Father Stephan and said, "Will you please follow him?" The guard showed them to a conference room near the Secretary of State's office. The guard suggested that they be seated and make themselves comfortable. If they wished, coffee was on a small table in the corner of the room. Each man got a cup of coffee and sat on the couch.

Dick asked, "I wonder how long we are going to wait."

Father Stephan said, "Oh, I do not think it will be too long."

No sooner had he gotten the words out of his mouth than a side door opened and Cardinal Vellini walked in. Both men started to rise from the couch, but he gestured them to remain seated and said, "In lieu of the circumstances, let us keep this informal." He continued, "I have been looking forward to this moment with great expectation."

Dick noticed that he frowned slightly as he looked over Father Stephan. He looked at Dick and said, "You are probably not the one who has the same appearance as the Holy Father."

Then he turned to Stephan and said, "In spite of your dark hair, you must be the one."

Father Stephan rose and said, "Yes, Eminence, I am."

The Cardinal extended his hand, and introduced himself as did Father Stephan. Dick also rose and introduced himself. After a few moments, the Cardinal said, "Are you the one that is supposed to take—" and he held his sentence.

He continued, "Is that disguise permanent?"

Father Stephan said, "No. I can have it off in a matter of seconds."

The Cardinal got himself a cup of coffee and sat down opposite the two men. He looked at Father Stephan and said, "Tell me about yourself, please."

Father Stephan did. The Cardinal inquired as to the number of languages he could speak and with what fluency. He also questioned him about the Vatican operation.

When they were finished with their coffee, the Cardinal rose and said, "If you will please come with me I will take you to the Pope's apartment."

They walked down the hall and entered the apartment. The first room was a sitting room. It was luxurious in its simplicity. On the wall hung paintings of landscapes, a seascape and a beautifully done head of Christ. As Dick passed, the eyes seemed to follow him.

They walked into the bedroom that was off the hallway. The Cardinal pointed and said, "The bath is that way."

On the bed was the white cassock that the Pope usually wore, and white socks. The zucchetto, worn by the Pope on his head, lay nearby. On the floor at the side of the bed were three pairs of shoes; low cut, and made of very soft leather. As the Cardinal gestured toward them he said, "I was guessing at the shoe size. If these do not fit, we will arrange to get others."

Another side room was an office with a large desk. In a semicircle, facing the desk were four leather chairs. The wall behind the desk was covered with books. Again, Dick thought, "Simple, but beautiful."

The Cardinal said, "Two other Cardinals and I meet here weekly to bring the Pope up to date on all facets of operation with the Church and the Vatican."

He turned and walked out of the room, back toward the bedroom. The other two men followed. Cardinal Vellini said to Father Stephan, "I will leave you now and if you could, get out of your disguise, put on the cassock, try on the shoes and when you are ready will you please come back to the conference room. I will call Cardinals Burns and Salvemini to see their reactions."

Chapter 31

After Cardinal Vellini left the room and closed the door, Dick said to Father Stephan, "I will go down to the conference room and get your bag."

Dick walked down the hall, got the bag, and returned. He put it on a stand. Father Stephan took off his jacket, tie and shirt. He removed the fake glasses, put them in a case and inserted them in a pocket of his traveling bag. With his index finger, he took out the pads that made his face a little fuller. After he was finished, he said to Dick, "You know, I am surprised. I can really eat quite well with these things." He continued, "What do you think is going on, Dick?"

Dick said, "I think they are going to make you the Pope's double."

Father Stephan said, "Oh, Good Lord, I hope not. I am not the Pope-type."

Dick replied, "Well, Steph, anything for the church. You can do it, if necessary."

Father Stephan gathered up some clothing out of his bag and walked toward the bathroom. About 20 minutes later he came out in a T-shirt, with his suit pants still on. He walked over to the bed and looked down at the white cassock. He said, "I wonder what the Pope wears under this."

Dick said, "Underwear, I would suppose, and a pair of trousers."

Dick walked over to the bed, lifted up the cassock and helped Father Stephan put it on. Stephan looked at himself in a mirror and said, "It fits quite well."

Dick said, "You must do something with those pants. You can see them below the bottom of the cassock."

Father Stephan said, "Shall I roll them up?"

Dick said, "No, but did you bring along your tennis shorts?"

Father Stephan thought for a moment and then said, "Yes, I did," and he went over to the bag, got them and put on the athletic shorts.

"There," he said, "that is better." He put on the white socks and tried the shoes until he found a pair that fit well.

Dick said, "You should comb your hair the way Jim told you."

Stephan went over to the mirror and combed his hair in the style that the Holy Father had used. He then put on the little skullcap.

"There," he said, "how do I look?"

"Holy Father, you look great!"

Father Stephan chuckled and then said, "Well, shall we go back to the conference room?"

Dick said, "Okay, let's go for it. Now, in all respect, I will follow you."

When they got to the conference room, Dick knocked on the door that led to Cardinal Vellini's office. Cardinal Vellini came into the conference room followed by two other Cardinals. All three men stared at Father Stephan. Cardinal Burns said,

"I do not believe it."

Cardinal Salvemini said, "I feel like blessing myself."

All three of the Cardinals were startled at Father Stephan's amazing likeness to the Pope. Cardinal Vellini reached into a pocket and said to Father Stephan, "You will also need this." He produced the Pope's ring and put it on Father Stephan's finger. It fit perfectly.

"What do we do now?" asked Father Stephan.

"Well, the first thing," said Vellini, "we have to get used to calling you 'Holy Father' because that is imperative. No mistakes may be made. Come, sit, we have a briefing to do. First, this is Cardinal Salvemini. He is liaison with the Tribunal of the Sacred Roman Rota. He also is in charge of our civil court in Vatican

City, although the Italian government prosecutes most cases of criminal activity. Cardinal Burns is liaison with the Congregation of the Ceremonial. This group takes care of all special events and audiences. In addition, Cardinal Burns, because of his financial expertise, coordinates all the financial matters of the Vatican. Each department in our hierarchy has its own financial officer, but in the end they report to Cardinal Burns. Also, he oversees the activities of the Vatican Council. I am concerned with political and some ecclesiastical matters, but the Pope is the supreme head of the church. However, because of his activity with ecclesiastical matters, he delegates through us most of the rest of the operational procedures. We, however, through periodic meetings, keep him appraised of everything that is happening."

They talked for another half hour, explaining the operations of the Vatican. When there was a lull in the conversation, Father Stephan said, "Is there anything that the Pope does that is unusual or not known to many people?"

Cardinal Vellini said, "Yes, there is one thing. About once every two weeks, he likes to sneak out of the Vatican and go to a small church six blocks away to say Mass. The pastor at the church is an old friend from Poland."

Dick Rogers said, "Who goes with him?"

Cardinal Vellini thought for a moment, and then said, "I believe it is one of the Swiss guards."

Dick said, "What about security in the Vatican?"

Cardinal Vellini said, "We have the Swiss guards, the Noble guards and the Palatine guards and of course, the police force.

Dick asked, "How closely is the Pope guarded?"

Cardinal Burns said, "I do not believe it is a very close guarding, but he is watched."

Dick said, "You have heard about the potential assassination plot on the Holy Father?"

All three men nodded their heads yes. Dick said, "I notice people have identification badges. I would like one for myself, to be able to come and go as I please."

Cardinal Burns said, "We have already taken care of that."

Dick added, "I would like to have an additional seven such badges. We have brought with us from the United States, seven people who will act as a very special security force. One of them is a priest. The others are brothers. I cannot tell you how, but they all have great experience in this matter. At all times, we would like to have one of them near the Pope's apartment or near him as he moves about. They will be very unobtrusive and will blend in with the rest of the people. No one will ever know that these people are security."

Cardinal Burns said, "We will take care of it."

"Now for the business at hand," said Cardinal Salvemini, "tomorrow morning, as a test case, the Pope will receive for his first audience the governor, really the mayor, of Vatican City. He will report to the Holy Father. Then, later in the day, we have scheduled an audience with three Chinese nationals. These men are seeking assistance from the Holy Father. It seems in the northern province there have been several earthquakes in addition to a drought throughout the summer. They are short on food supplies. They probably want assistance from the church and may also want the Holy Father to take their case to the wealthier nations of the world for additional assistance. In return, I believe, they may open one of the Catholic churches in Beijing and let their Catholic citizens attend Mass. This is very important. I believe Cardinal Vellini will accompany the Holy Father."

Cardinal Vellini nodded his head yes.

"Well," said Vellini, "are there any questions?"

Father Stephan asked, "You really want me to replace the Pope?"

All three Cardinals nodded. "It is imperative. You see, at the present, His Holiness is in a hospital in the northern part of Italy, being prepared for surgery tomorrow. He is in need of a kidney transplant for which we have found a donor."

Dick asked, "What happens if he does not survive?"

Cardinal Vellini said, "We will face that if we come to it, but we are assured by his physicians that he will come through the surgery and regain his strength."

Father Stephan said, "I would like to have my friend and advisor," and he nodded toward Dick, "to be near me so that I can discuss matters with him. We are used to doing this."

Cardinal Vellini said, "An apartment has been prepared for him, and we will make sure that they bring his bags over from the hotel."

Dick said, "No, don't do that. I will sleep at the hotel and stay here during the day. It is important that I do this because I must be in contact with the head of the security people I mentioned."

Father Stephan said, "I think that is a good idea. I feel awkward about this. I probably cannot roam the halls, nor sneak into the kitchen and raid the refrigerator."

Cardinal Vellini smiled and said, "Holy Father, your wish is our command. If you feel like eating something, all you have to do is signal with the little bell in your apartment. Whatever you need will be provided."

Father Stephan said, "Thank you."

Cardinal Vellini looked at the other two Cardinals and said, "If there isn't anything else, we'll let His Holiness retire. Mr. Rogers, there will be a young man in the corridor who will escort you back to your hotel. He will be instructed to bring you back in the morning. All you need to do is tell him what time to pick you up. Our plan starts. May the good Lord be with us as we pray for a successful conclusion to this adventure."

Chapter 32

Father Jason got out of his car, walked up the stairs and into the Inn. Harry was sitting behind the bar reading his newspaper. When he heard the door close, he looked up, turned to Father Jason and said, "May I help you, Father?"

Father Jason said, "I hope so. I would like to contact a man named Rene."

Harry said, "He has been busy this week. You are the second person who has asked for him."

Father Jason said, "Did the first man make contact?"

Harry said, "Yes, he did." Harry continued, "Father, are you sure you want to meet this person? He is not one whom I would associate with a priest."

Father Jason said, "All I am doing is following some instructions."

Harry said, "Very well. I will try him now." He went to the phone and dialed the number, talked for a few seconds, and hung up. He came back and told Father Jason that Rene would be at the Inn around noon. "I was lucky. I talked to Rene directly. Father Jason arranged to stay at the Inn for the night.

After breakfast the next morning, Father Jason went out on the veranda and watched the scenery for a while. Along the dock he noticed a boat tied up. Two men were working on something on the deck. He decided to go over and see what it was. As he approached the boat, he said good morning to the two fishermen in French, their native language. One of the men invited him aboard. They were working on a small motor. One man explained that the motor had no strength, and it was usually used to power the winch that hauled their fishing net aboard the boat.

Father Jason was mechanically inclined and decided that he would like to watch the two as they repaired the motor. One man was quite vehement in his opinion that the problem with the motor was a stuck valve; the other was just as solid that it was something wrong with the piston and they were not getting enough compression. Jason was amused at their good-natured bickering. It took the two men a considerable length of time to strip away the brackets and other parts of the engine before they could get at the head. They worked slowly and seemed to be in no great hurry to finish the job. Without the engine working, they could not go fishing, so this was their project for the day. From time to time they stopped their efforts and got into discussions about various things. Father Jason questioned them as to their lives as fishermen. Both agreed they really enjoyed life and for the most part, they told him they did well and were able to provide comfortably for their families. Jason discovered that the two men were brothers and had inherited the boat from their father. The older of the two men took a watch from his pocket, looked at it and said to his brother, "Where has the time gone. It is time to eat."

Jason looked at his watch and saw that it was approaching noon. He kept watching the Inn to see if any cars drew up. The older of the two men went to the rear of the boat, took hold of a stout hawser that was over the rail, and gently pulled it up. At the end of the hawser was a wine bottle covered with fish net and securely tied. He undid the string and brought the bottle to where the other two were seated. The younger man reached into a box and pulled out a large paper package. They each wiped their hands thoroughly on some clean cloths, then unfolded the paper bundle and produced sausage, cheese and bread. The older man poured three glasses of wine. They invited Father Jason to lunch.

Over the meal the men asked many questions about life in the United States and what Father Jason knew about fishing. He had to admit he knew very little, but described a visit he had once had to the coast of Maine. When lunch was over and the wrappings and glasses were cleared away, the two men removed the head of the engine and saw the cause of their trouble. The one man pointed and gleefully said, "See, a burnt valve. That is our problem."

The other chuckled and said, "You are right."

He walked over to a box and started to rummage through bits of parts and pieces. At last he came up with a valve and said, "Here, this is the answer."

Father Jason said, "You carry your own supplies with you?"

The older man said, "That we must. There are no stores around here."

Father Jason glanced up and saw a black car pull into the parking area of the Inn. He said to the two men, "I see that the man with whom I have business has arrived. I must leave you. Thank you very much for allowing me to participate with you in this interesting morning, and thanks for the lunch."

The younger man said, "This will take us a couple of hours. Would you like to go out with us when we test the motor?"

Jason said he would enjoy that very much. He got up and started to walk toward the Inn. A man in a dark suit was seated in one of the rocking chairs, smoking. Father Jason approached him and said, "Rene?"

The man looked Jason over from head to foot and answered, "Yes."

He then continued, "What does a priest want with me?"

Father Jason sat next to Rene and said, "Quite simply, I wish to talk about George."

Rene said, "George?" in a questioning manner.

Father Jason turned in his chair, looked directly into Rene's eyes and said, "Let us not play games. I know all about George. I know that he took a contract to assassinate the Pope and I would like to talk to him face to face."

Rene said, "That is impossible." Rene continued, "I can give him your message and get back to you. What do you want to tell him?"

"Just this," said Father Jason, "If he attempts to carry out the contract, whether he is successful or not, he will be followed to the ends of the earth and no place will be safe for him. His career will come to a sudden and violent end."

Rene looked almost startled by these words and he said, "That is very strong language for a priest, is it not?"

"No," said Father Jason, "because we are talking about the supreme head of a church, something we hold near and dear."

"All right," said Rene, "I will take your message to him. You can expect me back here about dusk."

Rene got up, walked to his car, got in and drove off. As Father Jason watched the car disappear down the road, he thought: "I am very glad that Giovanni gave me the automatic. This might get touchy." He looked back to the dock and decided to enjoy the afternoon because he did not know what the evening would bring.

When he got back to the fishing boat, the two men were just completing the engine repair. They seemed quite pleased with themselves for having accomplished their job. When the last bracket was in place and the engine and winch looked as if they would be operational, the younger man pushed the starter button. The engine coughed several times but then started to chug away. He turned to Father Jason and said, "Let's test it." The older man started the main engines to drive the boat out into the bay. Father Jason cast off the stern mooring while the younger man untied the forward rope from the piling. Very soon, they were chugging their way out into the bay.

When they were a considerable distance out, the younger man said to Father Jason, "Would you like to try to catch a few fish?"

Jason said, "Why not?"

The younger man went to a locker and pulled out a jacket and a pair of coveralls. Jason took off his suit jacket and his collar and put on the work clothes.

Suspended over the stern of the boat was a framework in the shape of an inverted U. The framework was attached on a hinge-like structure to the stern. A rope ran from the top of the U to pulleys mounted on a boom and then down to the winch. The young man pushed forward a lever on the winch and they dropped the framework slowly so that it was parallel to the water. The young man joined Jason at the stern of the boat, and both started to play out the pile of netting that was on the deck.

When they got to the end, Father Jason noted that the ends of the net were weighted so that it would sink into the water. A long rope attached both sides of the net to the boat. The man in the pilothouse slowed the forward motion of the boat and as they moved forward, the net acted as a scoop to catch any fish that might be in its path. After a while they cut the engines and the boat moved ahead slowly on its own inertia. When the boat was almost at a halt the younger man said, "Well, let's try it."

Father Jason on one side, the man on the other side, started to pull in the net. Jason could feel the net getting heavier and heavier. When they got to a certain point the young man said, "We will stop here." He tied off both sides of the net with ropes secured to eyebolts. He suggested that Father Jason should move away. Bending over, he picked up two panels from the deck. Father Jason noted a small hold. The man went back to the winch, moved the lever, and slowly the framework rose above the water, lifting the net up with it. Suddenly fish started to slip from the net down into the hold. When the framework was as high as it could go, the man pushed the lever forward and came aft. He and Jason continued to pull the net until it was empty of fish. Several fish had been caught in the mesh and had to be retrieved by hand. The man looked at Jason and said, "You are good luck, Father. I did not think we would catch anything. It is very late in the day, so this catch will go to the townspeople." He yelled to the man in the pilothouse who again started the engines and headed back to the dock. When they had tied up, Jason took off his work clothes and at a small basin on the side of the pilothouse, washed his hands very thoroughly. He put on his collar and his coat.

Again he was Father Jason. He thought to himself: "this is probably the way Peter and the other apostles caught fish. Well, I have done something new, something enjoyable."

He thanked the two men for his experience, leaped up onto the dock and walked back to the Inn. He went to his room, showered, and changed clothes. He came back downstairs to the dining area to have his dinner. When he was finished with his meal, he took his coffee and sat at the bar so that he could talk to Harry. Father Jason and Harry swapped many military stories. They talked for several hours. It was now completely dark outside. When the door opened, Harry looked at the person coming in and nodded his head to Jason. Jason turned on his stool and saw Rene. Rene suggested that he wanted him to come outside. When they were out on the porch and out of the range of Harry's hearing, Rene said, "Come on, follow me. The man you want to see is behind, on the next street."

Rene led him down a small alley between two buildings. The farther they walked, the darker it got. Father Jason rubbed his hand along the wall of the building to orient himself. Suddenly, a light came on in one of the rooms. It completely illuminated Rene. He had turned and was standing there with a pistol pointed at Father Jason. Jason thought, "What a perfect target with the light behind me." He could not do much, not even reach for his gun.

Rene said, "Priest, you have involved yourself in something that is not your business. You will pay for it. I will even bless you."

With his left hand he made the sign of the cross in the air. Before he could finish there was the ear-piercing blast of a shotgun. The full load caught Rene in the stomach and the chest and he went down to the ground backwards. Father Jason moved forward to where Rene lay. He knelt down and could see by the man's eyes that he was still alive. He gave him absolution and blessed him. Rene's head fell to the side and he was dead. Father Jason reached down and closed his eyes. He then stood up and turned toward a shadow on the side of the building and asked, "Who are you?"

The voice came back, "I am your guardian angel."

Jason responded questioningly, "Guardian angel?"

"Yes," said the man, "I was sent to watch over you. I have been with you ever since you got off the boat."

"But who sent you," asked Jason?

"Don Giovanni," said the voice.

"May I ask your name?" said Jason.

"Yes," said the voice, "it is Angelo."

"Well Angelo, I thank you. Nevertheless, won't you get into deep trouble here when the police arrive? Surely they heard the shot."

Angelo said, "Do not worry about it. There are no police in this town, and before long there will be no evidence that anyone came to a bad end. In about 15 minutes all traces will be gone but do not ask me where or how."

"Come, let us go back to the street," he continued. As they got to the lighted street, Angelo held out a little piece of paper and said, "Here is an address. After this guy talked to you, I had him followed. I think you will find your man on the second floor, rear apartment. Now, why don't you go in and have a drink and get a good night's sleep. You will need it for tomorrow."

The men shook hands and Father Jason thanked him again for saving his life. As Father Jason started to enter the Inn, he looked toward the side of the building and he saw several dark figures joining Angelo. He stood for a moment and thought, "I am glad I do not have to do the job that they are going to do. How lucky I was to be able to talk to Don Giovanni."

He entered the Inn and walked to the bar where Harry sat reading. Harry looked up and said, "You look like you need a drink."

Father Jason said, "Maybe a cup of coffee."

"And a small drop of brandy," added Harry.

Jason nodded his head. Harry poured two cups of coffee and added brandy to each. The men slowly sipped their drinks and chatted. Nothing was said about the shotgun blast. After about an hour, Father Jason said, "Well, I think I'll go up to bed."

Harry said, "Have a good night's sleep. I'm going to be closing soon."

Chapter 33

It was decided that Cardinal Vellini would guide Father Stephan through his appointments for the day. Cardinals Salvemini and Burns with Dr. Santos left for the hospital so that they would be there for the Pope's operation. The three men were seated in a glass-encased amphitheater above the operating room. They could observe everything that took place below them. Dr. Santos said he would try to describe the operation in lay people's terms. He added that he could turn on a closed circuit TV so that they would have a clear picture of the operation. Both men declined.

Shortly after they seated them, two men wheeled the Pope into the operating theater. A nurse dipped a gauze pad held with forceps into a stainless steel bowl that contained a reddish brown solution. Dr. Santos explained that this was an antiseptic. The nurse covered the lower left quadrant of the abdomen with this solution. When she was finished, she took blue cloths out of a sterile pack and placed them across the Pope's body so that they exposed only the swabbed skin area. The anesthesiologist put a plastic clip with a wire leading to a machine on the Pope's index finger. Dr. Santos explained that this would give an oxygen level readout on the machine. Circular discs were placed around the Pope's chest, again with leads going to the machine. Also, a blood pressure cuff was placed on the Pope's right arm. Dr. Santos explained all of this would give the anesthesiologist readings on respiration, blood pressure, heart monitoring and pulse. He explained that the bags hanging from the stand were antibiotics plus a solution of salts that were necessary. A small tube was placed in the Pope's neck. He said this was for monitoring and, if needed, for the injection of an anesthetic medication. Dr. Santos explained further that a combination of chemicals and gas was to be used as an anesthesia, and throughout the operation the anesthesiologist would monitor the Pope's vital signs.

Dr. Santos also said that there were more people available here than were really necessary, again, as a precaution.

When the Pope was under the anesthetic, the surgeon and his assistant walked in. They were completely gowned, and had scrubbed their hands thoroughly. The nurse helped each of them put on his rubber gloves. The operation was about to commence. Dr. Santos told them that the same routine was happening in the next room where they would remove Father O'Connor's kidney. He went on to explain that they would make an incision, the muscles parted, until they exposed the kidney.

Cardinal Burns asked, "What does the kidney look like?"

Dr. Santos replied, "Well, it is reddish brown and is shaped like a bean."

Santos stated that when they expose the kidney, they would tie off and cut the renal artery and vein, as would be the tube leading to the bladder. He continued,

"Taking out the kidney is really the easier part. Putting another one in takes more time."

"What about rejection," asked Cardinal Salvemini?

"Well, we have drugs to counter the rejection," said Dr. Santos, "and here there is a four-point match that is almost perfect. We are really not concerned about rejection."

In their conversation the three men lost track of what was happening down below and it seemed, not long after, an individual came from the next room, carrying what looked like a stainless steel bowl covered with a cloth. Dr. Santos said,

"Well, there is the new kidney."

Cardinal Burns said, "I am glad they cover it. I do not think I could take that."

Dr. Santos told them that probably the kidney would not be in the same position as it was originally. The surgeon would make a little pocket and reconnect the artery, the veins and the tubes. This connection had to be done very carefully so that there were no leaks.

Several hours later, the surgeon and his assistant turned and walked away from the table. Cardinal Burns could see that they had covered the wound with a dressing and that they were putting a sheet and a blanket over the Pope and they also were disconnecting some leads going into the machines. Dr. Santos said, "Well, now he will go into an intensive care recovery room and all we have to do is wait."

"When can we see him?" asked Cardinal Salvemini.

Dr. Santos replied, "Well, that depends on many factors. It will be several hours and even then he will not be completely lucid."

Dr. Santos suggested the Cardinals return to the Vatican and said he would keep in contact with them by phone. It would be best if they waited until the next day to see the Pope.

When they returned to the Vatican, they reported all the details to Cardinal Vellini and Father Stephan.

Early in the morning Cardinal Vellini had met with Father Stephan in anticipation of an appointment with the Governor of the Vatican. The Governor, in reality, was the Mayor and although the Vatican is an independent state approximately one-sixth of a square mile in area, it is also a complete city. Vellini told him that the Governor is in charge of running the city-state. He told Father Stephan that the Vatican has all the departments that any other city would have. Besides utilities, there is the printing of stamps, the post office, and banks, even the printing of license plates.

Vellini said, "You know, we even have our own railroad. It is only about 300 yards long and is connected to the Italian railway. Nevertheless, it brings in all the freight, all the materials used to operate the Vatican."

He continued, "When most people think of the Vatican, they think of the Pope and the clergy dashing around, doing the business of the Lord. However, it is more than that. Not many people think of the Vatican in the mundane terms that I have outlined. We have a population of approximately 1,000—people doing all kinds of work. The Pope, of course, is in complete charge and responsible for everything. His major concern is with ecclesiastical matters and he delegates the rest to others. Of course, from time to time, as with the Governor, His Holiness is brought up to date on all facets of operation."

When Cardinals Salvemini and Burns had finished with their description of the Pope's operation, Cardinal Burns asked, "How did the appointment go with the Governor?"

Cardinal Vellini said, "Splendidly. The Governor had no idea, at all, that he was not reporting directly to His Holiness. I must say Father Stephan did extremely well. He asked the appropriate questions and was in command of the situation throughout the encounter."

Father Burns said, "Excellent. Now, we do have a meeting with representatives of the Chinese government this afternoon, do we not?"

Cardinal Vellini said, "Yes. I have briefed Father Stephan on their intent and if he does as well with them as he did with the Governor, things should go very smoothly."

Father Stephan suggested that they use one of the smaller rooms to receive the Chinese representatives. He said, "Because of their beliefs, or rather non-beliefs, I think it would be better if we used as little pomp and ceremony as we can."

Cardinal Vellini responded, "I think that is a very good idea, Father. We do not want to make them uncomfortable."

Later that afternoon, Cardinal Vellini, Father Stephan and an interpreter were seated in a small conference room. The chairs had been placed almost in a circular fashion. Father Stephan looked at the interpreter with a little twinkle in his eyes and thought, "Maybe I will not need you. I can probably pull this off myself."

When the door opened, the three men stood. Cardinal Vellini looked at Father Stephan and frowned as he thought that the

Pope should remain seated. Father Stephan looked at him and said,

"My dear Cardinal, it is a matter of face—saving face."

Father Stephan knew that Cardinal Vellini did not know what he was talking about, and realized he would have to explain later. Father Stephan had not only studied the language but the culture of the Chinese people.

One of the Swiss guards escorted three men into the room. They were impeccably dressed in dark suits, white shirts and ties, instead of the usual Chinese mode of attire. Father Stephan took this as a sign of respect. The interpreter introduced them. Mr. Lee was the smallest and the thinnest and probably the youngest of the three. The next was Mr. Chen. He was rather tall for a Chinese person. The last was Mr. Chang, gray-haired and the oldest of the group. Father Stephan took him to be the leader. However, he knew that in their conversations he should include the other two through eye contact. The three bowed just enough so as not to be discourteous. They were stiff in their approach. Their expressions changed greatly when Father Stephan greeted them in their native language, and he suggested with a sweep of his hand for them to be seated. When Mr. Chang was in his chair, Father Stephan then sat. Again, in their own language, he asked if they had had a pleasant journey from Beijing. After a pause he asked if they would like to join him for tea. Mr. Chang said yes.

Father Stephan took up a small bell that was on a table next to his chair and rang it. Presently a young man, who was obviously Chinese, came into the room pushing a cart. The cart was black and well lacquered and upon the top sat a beautiful, delicate, bone china tea set. The young man put the measured amounts of tea into the pot, and into this he poured steaming water. He took up a bamboo whisk and with deliberate motion, stirred the concoction. After a moment, he tapped the whisk on the side of the bowl and put it back on the table. He poured each cup of tea and served those around the room. The interpreter declined because he was not a part of the important group.

As they enjoyed their tea, Father Stephan and members of

the Chinese delegation made small talk. Mr. Lee complimented Father Stephan on the quality of the tea. Father Stephan replied that it was China black and imported through Hong Kong. This seemed to please his Chinese guests.

Cardinal Vellini thought this conversation was very frivolous and could not understand why they did not get to the point. Father Stephan thought that he would have to explain later to the good Cardinal the courtesies of doing business in China.

When the tea was finished, Father Stephan glanced at each man before him and said, "What may we do for you?"

Chang was the first one to respond and explained that they were there at the urging of Bishop Wong in Beijing. He added that the northern provinces of China had not only had earthquakes but also a long drought and there were thousands of hungry people. He was seeking the assistance of the Holy One to help. After Chang was finished, Father Stephan put the fingers of both hands together as if in prayer and said, "We will be happy to assist. I believe we can do this almost immediately. In addition, I would be happy to contact the heads of the more wealthy nations and seek their assistance in the name of the people of northern China."

The faces of the three Chinese representatives broke into broad smiles. Father Stephan continued, "I will leave you with the good Cardinal Vellini, our Secretary of State, and he will work out details with you. Of course, we will assign an appropriate person to be liaison with Beijing. If it were not for the fact that Bishop Wong was under house arrest, we could use his services also."

Chang looked up in surprise and said, "Since his church in Beijing has been reopened, he and his associates are presently free to come and go as they please."

Father Stephan thought, "Bingo. Score one. That means the priests are out of jail, the church is open and the Bishop is free to act as a bishop." Father Stephan said to Chang, "That is wonderful. The Bishop would be an excellent man to help us carry out this work."

Father Stephan rose and the three Chinese representatives followed suit. Father Stephan bowed slightly. The three bowed with more enthusiasm than when they first entered the room. Mr. Chang did something very unusual. He extended his right hand to grasp Father Stephan's and using both hands, shook Father Stephan's hand vigorously. He looked Father Stephan in the eyes and said, "Holy One, the people of China thank you and we thank you."

Father Stephan responded, "We are doing nothing more than helping our brothers and sisters. You are welcome."

The three men, the interpreter and Cardinal Vellini left the room. Father Stephan sat down for a moment and said a prayer. He thought, "In some small way I may have helped the Church again to be vital in the Chinese republic."

Chapter 34

George, the assassin, wandered around the Vatican. He was dressed informally and could pass as any other tourist admiring the paintings, sculptures and buildings. However, in reality, he was trying to develop a plan on how to assassinate the Pope. His efforts seemed futile. After two full days, he was no closer to his target than when he began. He was seated on one of the benches in the garden, smoking a cigarette. Suddenly he caught sight of a small vehicle that looked like a golf cart. It was enclosed and had a small space in back to carry tools. The man in this contraption had gone from one building to another, carrying a bag with what George assumed were his tools. He got an idea, got up from his bench, walked over and sat near the little cart. When the man came out of the building, George stood, smiled and nodded.

The man said, "Good afternoon."

George returned his greeting and said, "Tell me, what are you doing?"

The man smiled and responded, "You know, no one else has ever asked me that in all the years I have worked here in the maintenance department. People seem to only have eyes for the architecture, the paintings, the sculptures, and the gardens. We pass as if we were invisible."

George said, "Maybe that is because I have been looking for someone just like you."

George extended his hand, smiled and said, "My name is Sam Johnson."

The man took George's hand and said, "I am Pietro Santini." George said, "Where did get your American accent?"

Pietro responded, "When I was a young man I went to visit my uncle in New York, and he decided that I should stay there and get my education. I went to a technical school where I learned my trade, and then came back and got a job in the Vatican maintenance department."

George said, "Pietro, I know you are busy now. Is there a place where we could meet after you are finished your day's work? I would like to buy you a drink and discuss an idea I have with you."

Pietro told him of a small cafe several blocks from the Vatican, and they arranged to meet when Pietro was finished.

George got to the cafe a little early and sat down at one of the small round tables placed on the sidewalk in front. He ordered a glass of wine and sipped it slowly. Not long after, he saw Pietro walking toward him. He smiled and said, "Sit. What will you have?"

Pietro also ordered a glass of wine. George moved a little closer to Pietro so as not to be overheard by other customers and he said, "Pietro, I am a freelance writer and I have an idea for a story that I think might sell. Would it be possible for me to accompany you during the day, sort of as your assistant? I could take notes for a story on the invisible people in the Vatican who make things work."

Using Pietro's own phrase challenged him and he smiled and said, "Yes, I think that could be arranged."

George said, "Of course I will pay you."

Pietro said, "That is not really necessary."

George said, "If I am going to make money, then I will pay you."

Pietro said, "Good."

They arranged to meet the next morning.

The following day, George met Pietro at the arranged place. They climbed into what George called the little golf cart. Pietro had a list of all the things he needed to do that day. The first stop was the Basilica of Saint Peter's where he had to change some light bulbs. Pietro parked the cart and they entered the Basilica through a side door. When they were inside, even George was impressed. The church was in the shape of a cross. Along its walls, though some areas were dimly lit, he could see altars and little chapels. He pointed to an area and said, "What's that, Pietro?"

Pietro responded, "Those are the tombs."

George said, "What do you mean, tombs?"

Pietro said, "Well, those are the tombs, I think, of church dignitaries, some royalty and some, I do not think anyone knows because there are no markings on them."

The place was really magnificent. Pietro said, "Come, I will show you something beautiful."

They walked along and came upon an area and there, delicately illuminated, was the Pieta. It had been sculpted by Michelangelo to represent the grieving Mother of Jesus after His death. Standing near it was a guard. Pietro acknowledged the guard's presence and it seemed that the guard knew him. Pietro said, "Isn't that beautiful?"

George answered, "Yes, it is."

Pietro said, "I have often been amazed at how the artist got the stone so smooth that it really looks like skin."

George asked, "Didn't somebody attack the statue with a hammer?"

Pietro said, "Yes, but due to the work of our excellent artists, you cannot even tell, can you?"

George said, "No."

They finished their job in the Basilica and went back to the cart. For most of the day, they fixed things—leaking pipes, dripping faucets, light switches, changing fuses—all kinds of minor repairs. George scribbled many observations in his notebook. Pietro thought they were notes for his article, when in reality they were nothing more than places of guards, times of changes of guards, who was where, and other information to help him in his task, but nothing really specific yet.

Chapter 35

Father Jason arose early. In spite of everything, he had a good night's sleep. He showered, dressed and packed his toilet articles in the travel bag. As he did so he thought that although Giovanni said he was retired, he still had one heck of an organization. The question that bothered him was how Angelo got to be here. He was sure he did not see the man on the boat coming over from Sicily. "Ah well, that is just a little piece in a much-larger puzzle."

He went downstairs, had breakfast, paid his bill, checked out, shook hands with Harry and thanked him for his hospitality. Harry said, "I hope everything goes well for you."

Father Jason said, "Thank you," and left the Inn.

The trip to Marseilles was uneventful and without much trouble he found the address for which he was looking. He pulled up to the curb, parked and looked around. The street was quiet. He got out of the car, locked it and casually walked to the door of the address on the paper. As quietly as possible, he opened it. A hallway led straight to the back of the house. He climbed the set of stairs to his left, trying to keep his full weight to the side of the stairs to prevent a squeak. When he got to the top he continued toward the back and stood in front of the doorway leading into the apartment described to him. Very slowly and cautiously he tried the door. It was locked. From his pocket he pulled out a leather packet. He opened it, looked at the lock and then chose one of the little metal instruments inside the packet. It looked like a thin skeleton key. He got down on one knee, carefully inserted the key, and turned it very gently until he heard a click. He drew his gun out of the holster and held it, pointing upward. He was about to stand up and try to open the door when two bullets came through the door, imbedding themselves in the wall behind him. He thought, thank God I was smart enough to kneel down to open this. The bullets had passed about 8 inches above his head. If he had been standing, they would have caught him in the chest. He pointed the gun toward the door and fired three quick shots. He heard a sound, got up and swung the door open, pointing his gun out in front of him, in a defensive stance. He heard a noise to his left and cautiously rounded the partition that led into the kitchen. The window leading to the back of the house was open. There were no other exits out of the room so he moved quickly to the window. He could see the back of a man running toward the alley. He raised his gun and was about to fire when a high bush obscured the man. However, three children ran into the alley, so Father Jason did not fire. He put his gun back into the holster and said, "Not this time, but I will get you."

He glanced down at the windowsill. There were droplets of red blood. Father Jason thought he must have nicked the man, but not enough to do any real damage.

George ran down the alley to the street, turned right and walked briskly. While doing so, he wrapped a handkerchief around his hand where the bullet had grazed the flesh. There was no great damage but the wound stung badly. As he went, he thought, "It could not be the priest Rene told me about, or could it? I must be careful and watch every step."

Chapter 36

The following morning George met Pietro again. After their meeting, Pietro said, "You are in for a treat. We have several jobs to do in the Vatican castle. You will meet all types of people. You will probably also see some top people of Vatican City. If we are working and a Cardinal or a Bishop comes down the hall, we move to the wall but keep on with what we are doing. During working hours we do not have to kneel or pay the respect that is usually due these people. Again today I will point out the regular workers and tell you what they do."

George said, "Thanks a lot. I will really get a good deal of material for my article."

They continued over to the Vatican castle. George looked up and said, "Boy, this is some building!"

Pietro said, "Well, it is really several connected buildings."

George said, "How have you ever found your way through these?"

Pietro said, "When I first started, I had to ask many questions. We are going up to the third floor to the Secretary of State's offices. We have to meet his secretary, and then install an additional electric line for a new computer."

When they got up to the offices and checked in, the secretary told Pietro what was needed. He had almost everything in his tool bags, and he and George started to work. After about an hour and a half George said, "Where can I smoke?"

Pietro said, "Not in the building. Come on, we will pretend we have to go get more materials."

Pietro led George down a long hallway and George noticed two guards. He thought this was unusual. When he asked Pietro about it, Pietro said, "We are right near the Pope's private apartment."

As they passed the guards, Pietro nodded and greeted each of them. He obviously knew them very well, and they knew him. The one who spoke English said to Pietro, "Going for a cigarette?" and Pietro nodded yes. He signaled the other guard and said to Pietro, "I will join you."

They walked down the hall where George was surprised to see an elevator. They took it all the way down to the ground floor and went out a door into a garden area.

George offered each of the two men one of his cigarettes, and they accepted. As they sat and smoked, George made small talk with the guard, asking him about his job, how long he had worked, how he got the job and all sorts of unimportant questions. George said to the guard finally, "Do you often see the Pope?"

"Oh, once in awhile," replied the guard.

"I will bet he does not leave the building very much, does he?"

The guard responded, "Oh yes he does. He goes to the Basilica, the Sistine Chapel, and has his appointments in various rooms in the castle. Yes, he goes out. In fact," said the guard, "I really should not tell you this, but one of his favorite jaunts is usually Wednesday morning. He goes over to the small church several blocks from here to say the six o'clock mass."

George's ears perked up and he said, "I will bet he is heavily guarded, isn't he?"

"Oh, no. We have guards all over. However, he only goes with one other person, sometimes two."

"Six o'clock mass on Wednesdays, you say, huh? Why does he do that?"

"I never really got to ask him," the man said, laughingly. "However, I think it is his way of being an ordinary priest for about an hour. I probably would do the same thing if I were in his position."

They smoked and talked. When they had finished their cigarettes, Pietro and George returned to their duties. George helped Pietro all that day and decided he should come back the next. So as not to be too obvious, when he finished work with Pietro the following day, George stuck out his hand and said, "Well, with all your help, I have enough material to do a good article."

George pressed five one hundred dollar bills into Pietro's hand. When Pietro looked down, he said, "Thank you very much. This has been an interesting experience. I hope you mention me in your article, but not by name."

George said, "Do not worry, you will be in the article anonymously. Thank you for all you have done!"

They parted.

Chapter 37

Father Jason was walking along the boulevard that traveled from the river all the way to the Basilica. The sight of St. Peter's always impressed him, as it loomed skyward as if it were sitting on a stage toward Heaven. On each side of the Basilica were semi-circular colonnades. Father Jason envisioned these as two arms slightly curved, extending outward to accept the masses. He thought, "What a magnificent structure, dedicated to the honor and glory of God, the largest Christian church in the world."

The Italians had built the first structure in 325 A.D. in the shape of a rectangle. They made it like the Roman meeting halls. The building was placed over what was believed to be the tomb of Saint Peter. About 1506 the original building was destroyed and then the construction started on the current Basilica. It took 150 years to complete it. There were a dozen different architects. Bernini and Michelangelo were the outstanding designers.

As Father Jason entered the piazza, he noticed a group of men in brown robes. Like any other group of clergy tourists they were admiring the structure of the colonnades. Father Jason walked over to them and each in turn greeted him. They were the brothers from the monastery back in the United States. From all outward appearances they looked like any other brothers or monks who might be in Vatican City. However, on the sleeves of each was a small red shield. One of the men handed Father Jason a package that he slipped into his belt. He knew the package contained a weapon and a small radio. From his suit jacket, Jason took a piece of paper containing a diagram. He informed the brothers of the Pope's usual Wednesday morning mass at a local church. This information he had received from Dick who acted as liaison between Father Stephan and himself. Dick was a welcome visitor in Father Stephan's quarters where there was a free-flow of information. Father Jason gave each man a number corresponding to a place where each one would act as security around the church. Four of them would be on the outside; two would be in a parked car approximately half a block from the church, so that if they needed fast transportation they would have it.

After some discussion, the group broke up and walked off either separately or in pairs. Father Jason decided to wander around the Vatican some more, to familiarize himself so that he could act in case of an emergency.

Cardinals Vellini, Burns and Salvemini were having lunch with Father Stephan in the Pope's private quarters. They were discussing the audiences and meetings that Father Stephan, acting as the Pope, had over the last several days. Vellini stated that Father Stephan had done extremely well. However, he was a little bewildered about the meeting with the Chinese until Father Stephan had explained the cultural niceties of their way of doing business. Cardinal Burns said that His Holiness was recovering better than had been expected, and it should not be too long before he could come back to the Vatican Palace. Father Stephan said with a broad smile on his face, "I will be happy when that occurs. This job is just a little too much for me. I do not know how the man puts up with everything he has to do. The responsibility is overwhelming."

Cardinal Vellini said, "Yes it is, but he seems to thrive on it."

"Well," said Cardinal Burns, "according to Dr. Santos, it will probably not be much longer before your job is finished."

Father Stephan said, "I will be glad to get back to the archives and finish what I started a long time ago. Never in my life did I realize that someday I would try to fill the shoes of the Pope."

"You are doing very well," said Cardinal Vellini, "very well indeed."

Cardinal Salvemini looked at Father Stephan and asked, "What does your friend Dick have to tell you about the assassination attempt?"

Father Stephan responded, "One of his men actually came in contact with the assassin and, he believed, wounded the man slightly. We have a good idea who he is and Dick has added to the security force. Hopefully," continued Father Stephan, "we can trap the assassin and by that eliminate the threat to the Pope."

"Aren't you putting yourself in jeopardy," asked Cardinal Vellini?

"Maybe," responded Father Stephan, "but I have all the faith in the world in Dick's people." Father Stephan thought to himself, "Wouldn't these men be surprised if they actually knew who the security force was."

Chapter 38

Beau and Bob pulled into the driveway next to the rectory of St. Anthony's. They walked up the front steps and rang the bell. The door was answered by Father Mike who cheerfully said, "Gentlemen, good to see you. Come on in."

They followed him down the hall to his office. After they were seated, Father Mike asked, "What is new on the case?"

"Quite a bit," responded Beau, and he and Bob filled Father Mike on all the details about O'Neill.

"He was a real nut case," said Bob. "We really investigated his background, and by chance we found he might have been responsible for the killing of two nuns in Buffalo, New York. If the murderer had not been killed, he probably would have gone on with his vendetta against nuns. We have a very good idea why he did this, but there is nothing that we can really prove. As far as the person who shot O'Neill, we have no idea whom that would be. There was not one clue that we could use—no footprint, no shell casing, nothing. We really believe he could have been a professional."

Father Mike asked, "What would a professional be doing guarding the nuns?"

Beau said, "We really do not know, Father, but someone could have hired him or her to protect them."

"So, what are you going to do," asked Father Mike?

Bob said, "We are going to close the case and consider it justifiable homicide, which it really was. We feel if O'Neill hadn't been stopped, he would have continued with his vendetta and Lord only knows how many others he would have killed."

"Well, I guess that is it," said Beau, as both he and Bob rose to leave.

Father Mike got up from his chair, and shook the hands of both men as he walked them to the door. As they were going out, he said, "Gentlemen, if you are ever in the neighborhood, I would be happy to have you stop in for a cup of coffee."

Both men said they would and walked to their car. As Father Mike walked back to the office, he thought, "Ah, the secrets of life. We will never know who saved the sister, but at least now we can return to normalcy and will not have to be afraid of every shadow."

Chapter 39

Father Stephan arose early, dressed and was ready to go to the Chapel and celebrate Mass. He went down the elevator, out the back door, and was met by Father Jason and Dick as they had arranged. They walked the few blocks to the church. Father Stephan and Dick entered the back door to the sacristy. Father Jason had told them not to come out until he appeared after the Mass. Father Jason walked around the church and talked to each of the men stationed in their assigned posts. He clicked on the radio and talked to the man in the car. He believed everything was set but somehow had a foreboding that even the best-laid plans might go wrong.

Father Stephan was delivering a short homily in Italian. He looked over at the congregation and noticed that most of the worshipers seemed to be working people who had stopped to hear Mass on the way to their jobs. He gave no thought to the assassin. Outside, one of the brothers was standing with his back to the wall on the right side of the church. As he stood there in the shadows, he noticed a man dressed in black approaching. He was not sure whether he was a priest or not. As the man approached, he challenged him to stop. Without a sound the man fired his pistol. The bullet struck the brother in the right shoulder. The force thrust him back against the wall where he hit his head, knocking him unconscious. He slipped to the ground. The man continued across the front of the church and up an alleyway on the left-hand side.

Father Jason lifted the radio to his mouth and said, "Check in by number." Each of the men responded in number. Seconds later, there was a call from number six. "Brother Alfonse has been shot. He's down but not dead." Father Jason replied, "Use the car and take him to Dr. Philippe. It's all set up."

Father Jason looked at his watch. He could see the dial plainly now that the sky had begun to brighten. He noted that Mass would soon be over, and he walked slowly across the back of the church, into the door leading into the Sacristy.

Not long after the man in black had shot the brother and walked toward the alley, a little old lady came out of the church door. She was plainly dressed. She looked rumpled. Her hair was straggly under her broad-brimmed hat. Her cotton stockings were wrinkled. Across her left shoulder was a long canvas strap attached to a bag, dangling from her right side. She had her right hand in the bag as if to protect any valuables that might be contained there. She walked around and down the alley that the man in black had taken, walking slowly and quietly in her rubber-soled shoes.

Father Jason approached the corner of the churchyard near the Rectory door. He was horrified. Everything seemed to be moving in slow motion. Father Stephan, followed by Dick, had not waited, but was coming out into the alley. To his right, Father Jason could see a man in black pointing a pistol at Father Stephan. Father Jason drew his own gun, pointed it at the man, and just as he pulled the trigger there was a loud shot. Standing not 10 feet away, in the shadows, was the little old lady. The bottom of her bag had been completely blown out and the blast from the sawed-off shotgun had hit the assassin in the chest. Father Jason took three hurried steps. The man had fired and the bullet had hit the Pope. The woman spoke to Jason in a deep, baritone voice. She said, "Jason, this is Angelo. Get these people out of here before the cops come. I am not sure who hit him first, you or me, but he is dead."

The blast from the assassin's bullet had hit Father Stephan right over his heart. He had been forced backward into the arms of Dick and both fell to the ground. Father Stephan was lying there in Dick's arms.

Father Jason knelt. He could see the hole in the cassock. He said, "Good Lord, I think the Pope is dead."

Father Stephan lay there and after a few seconds he took a deep breath and opened his eyes. He said, "Help me up, I think I have either a bruised or a broken rib."

Jason was astounded. He and Dick helped Father Stephan up and walked slowly back to the Vatican Palace and the Pope's apartment.

In the apartment, Dick said to Father Stephan, "Let us get that cassock off and check the damage."

Father Stephan took off the cassock and to Father Jason's amazement, Father Stephan was wearing a bulletproof vest.

"Where did you get that," he asked?

Dick responded, "Oh, I got it from one of my Army buddies and decided to improve the Pope's mode of dress."

There was a big red welt on Father Stephan's chest. Dick said, "Looks like you only bruised your rib. You will be all right."

Father Jason seemed to be a bit bewildered. He said to Dick, "Something is wrong here. When the Pope was down on the ground with you, you kept calling him Stephan. Never have I heard that name before."

Father Stephan looked at Jason and said, "Father, I believe we can tell you the dark secret, and because of what we know about you, we can trust you. I am not the Pope. I am a stand-in. The Pope has had to undergo major surgery, and he is recuperating nicely. The Powers that Be felt that someone like me had to be present to maintain the status quo of the Church and keep the wheels grinding away as they should."

Chapter 40

Manny Salvador was at home. His family had gone on vacation, and he was alone. He had taken a shower, had changed and was trying to decide where to go to have his dinner. The doorbell rang and when he answered it, standing before him was a priest, with his round hat in his hand. It was obvious to Manny that this priest was not an American. The priest extended his hand and said, "I am Father Giuseppe Ventre." Just when this man was introducing himself, the *real* Father Ventre was sitting at the church organ practicing some hymns that he enjoyed.

The man continued, "I am from Sicily and bring you greetings from your Uncle Dominick, who is a good friend of mine. I am here in the United States to attend a conference and I will be leaving here tomorrow morning. Your uncle asked me to call upon you and take you out to dinner on his behalf."

"How is Uncle Dominick," asked Manny?

"Very well," said the priest.

Manny said, "I was just getting ready to go out for dinner."

The priest responded, "Your uncle has instructed me to take you to a restaurant that was his favorite when he was living here."

"Okay," said Manny, "let me turn off some lights. How did you get here?"

"A taxi cab," said the priest.

"Well, come on, we will take my car."

The restaurant was a small, typically Italian, neighborhood cafe.

"If you do not mind," said Father Giuseppe, "your uncle has given suggestions on what I should order."

"Be my guest," said Manny.

The dinner started with antipasto and had at least six courses, ending with coffee and brandy. The priest reached into his jacket pocket and produced a cigar case, offering one to Manny and said, "These, too, are from your uncle. He tells me you enjoy a good cigar. He gets them directly from Cuba, handmade, I understand."

Manny cut off the end of the cigar and lit it. He really enjoyed it with the coffee and brandy. When it was done, he looked at the priest and said, "I have not had a meal like this in years. I thank you, Father, and please convey my thanks to my uncle."

"Think nothing of it," said the priest.

"Now," said Manny, "where may I drop you?"

The priest asked if he could be taken and dropped near his hotel and Manny agreed.

As they came to the approximate area of his hotel, Father Giuseppe said, "Right here will be fine. I can walk a block or two as I need the exercise after that meal."

Manny said, "Yes, I could use some exercise too, but I think I will go home and turn in early."

"Very good," said the priest. He got out of the car, turned to walk away, then turned back to the car. He motioned for Manny to lower the window. Manny pushed a button and the window went down. The priest had his hand between the buttons of his cassock. Without Manny seeing, he withdrew a gun with a silencer. He said, "Oh yes, I forgot. Your uncle told me that I should take you out and see to it that you had a wondrous meal with good wine, finished off with coffee, brandy and a cigar."

Thoughts began flooding in Manny's head of the ritual assassinations. The potential victim was first wined and dined which put him in a good mood, and was then assassinated. The priest had his gun slightly below the window, and he said, "Oh yes, your uncle said you have been a very bad boy and that no one should try to kill the Pope. He hopes you have learned your lesson."

The priest lifted his arm, fired three times, hardly making a sound. Then he walked away down the street. He came to an alleyway between two buildings where he stripped off his cassock and hat and threw them in a dumpster. He walked half a block farther, wiping off the gun with a handkerchief, eliminating all traces of fingerprints, and dropped it into a sewer drain. An hour later he was aboard a plane heading back to Sicily.

Chapter 41

Several nights later, Fathers O'Connor, Stephan and Jason along with Dick were seated in a small conference room in the Vatican Palace. Cardinal Vellini had summoned them. They were talking over the events as they enjoyed their coffee. Father O'Connor had most of the questions, as he had been in the hospital during all of the events being discussed. When asked about his health, he said, "I am almost my old self and feel very good."

Suddenly a door opened and in walked the Pope, followed by Cardinal Vellini. The men in the room started to rise but the Pope motioned to them to stay seated. He said, "Gentlemen, this is an informal gathering. We would like to thank you for everything that you have done. First, Father O'Connor, we thank you for your kidney, so that we might continue in our appointed work. Anything that you want, we would be happy to grant."

Father O'Connor said, "Holiness, if possible, I would like to continue to do the work that I am doing."

The Pope said, "Granted." He looked at Father Stephan next and said, "Father, we thank you for filling our shoes, and we understand that you did a most admirable job."

He continued, "In fact, sometime when we need a rest, we might call upon you again."

Father Stephan looked at the Pope, rose, and with a big smile on his face, said, "Holiness, please know the job is too much for me."

The Pope smiled back. He then looked at Father Jason and said, "Father, I understand that you put your life in jeopardy several times to thwart the assassination attempts, and we are very grateful."

Then he gave his attention to Dick and said, "Richard, thank you for being a constant friend to Father Stephan and for helping him coordinate efforts between him and Father Jason. Likewise, you put yourself in jeopardy, and we thank you."

He continued, "We feel bad that a life had to be lost and we will pray for the soul of the man who was killed."

The Pope bowed to them and left the room. Father Stephan said, "Well, for three of us, it is back to the United States."

Epilogue

In the days that followed, the Pope gained in strength. He often thought about and prayed for the three men who came as strangers and became an integral part of his life.

Father O'Connor entered into his life in the Vatican with great enthusiasm. He felt no negative effects following the replacement of his kidney.

Father Stephan could not wait to get back to his home. The first thing he did was wash the black dye from his hair and get rid of the rest of his disguise. As he said to Dick, "I will be happy when my hair grows back in a month or two."

After he and Dick had taken care of the mail that had accumulated in their absence, they again set off for the monastery to continue their research.

For some reason, when Father Jason's plane landed and he took a cab into the city, he did not wish to return immediately to the monastery. Instead, the first night, he stayed at a motel. The next morning he got up, had breakfast, and decided to walk. As he walked along, not really paying any attention to where he was going, his mind was fixed on all that had happened. He thought about his friend in Sicily and how good it would be to be back there; about Dominick Giovanni and how Rene had almost trapped him in an alley; about shooting the attacker of the nun; about firing at the assassin. He was filled with mixed emotions. Sadness, because of taking a life; a melancholy joy about saving the Pope. When he finally looked up, he saw that he was standing in front of St. Anthony's Church. He turned and decided to go in.

Upon entering, he found the church was quiet and peaceful and only the light shining through the windows illuminated the interior. He knelt down in a pew to pray. He looked up and saw that a light was burning over the confessional. He thought, "The priest that is the pastor here must be an old timer as many people no longer use this type of confession."

Father Jason got up and walked slowly toward the confessional. He opened the door, closed it behind him and knelt down in the dark silence of the small cubicle. When he heard the small, shuttered door open, he visualized the priest on the other side of the cloth screen. Making the sign of the cross, he said, "Bless me, Father, for I have sinned."